ALIYAH

RICHARD MALMED

CONTENTS

ALIYAH

RICHARD MALMED

WORKBOOK PRESS LLC
187 E Warm Springs Rd,
Suite B285, Las Vegas, NV 89119, USA

Website: https://workbookpress.com/
Hotline: 1-888-818-4856
Email: admin@workbookpress.com

Ordering Information:
Quantity sales. Special discounts are available on quantity purchases by corporations, associations, and others. For details, contact the publisher at the address above.

ISBN-13:   978-1-956876-32-1 (Paperback Version)
                  978-1-956876-33-8 (Digital Version)

REV. DATE: 10.11.2021

Mrs. W

"Oh, Peter, this one's a beaut!" It was 10:00 a.m. and Angelina, my paralegal/legal secretary/she-wolf was referring to a new client waiting in the reception area. Our firm usually did just corporate or estate matters and I was the chief litigator. I was one of the few who went into court and tried cases. Because I had once been an assistant district attorney, I was referred criminal cases much to the dismay of my stuffy partners. I also took in some divorces because they paid quite well. But Angelina and I always welcomed a break from the heavy paperwork of the dull but money making part of the firm in corporate law.

"What have we got?" I say 'we' because Angelina always took a personal interest in our clients. If she liked them, she did extra research, chatted with them about their lives and generally held their hands while they stewed over some legal mess in their lives. She had three grown children, divorced her husband, and said that I was the only child she had left. Raised in the old Italian style, she fussed over me and protected me from who she, in here street-smart manner, decided were bad people. She also disinfected my phone and computer keyboard. Since I was raised in the suburbs, went to an Ivy League school and was book smart, she felt, and properly so, I was a naïf among those who might manipulate me.

"A big blowsy dame, smells of white wine and impoverished gentry. I've only done a short search." She was a whiz on the computer and looked forward to looking up details of people on the internet. Our law practice was her personal soap opera.

"Bring her back." I was ready to interview this new client and cleaned up my desk and took out the ubiquitous yellow pad all lawyers use to take notes. Unless this was a particularly personal matter, I usually had Angelina sit in and take notes. Her own personal take on the interviews was almost always helpful. She was raised in a blue collar neighborhood in a very traditional Italian family who did not believe in sending women to college. Her lack of book learning was more than compensated for by her native intelligence.

As previewed, Mrs. Witherspoon came into the office and took a seat.   She was indeed big and blowsy and smelled of inexpensive chardonnay. Maybe attractive in her day with large rosy cheeks, she was now plump with large breasts in a white blouse with a round collar and a circle pin. She wore a blue blazer and maroon slacks. The blouse was not ironed and seemed to have a few small stains. She did indeed smell of white wine, even at 10:00 in the morning and I thought cigarettes as well. She looked around my office, apparently judging me by my furnishings.

"Oh, I see you went to Yale. Let's see," she said squinting at my diploma, "did you know. . .' and she went on naming a few names of people she said she knew from her prep school. They were either younger, older, or from some exclusive group I didn't belong to. She was staking out her presumed place in society and wanted to let me know I was to respect her notion of herself. My experience was that these older moneyed people did look a bit worn around the edges, were mildly alcoholic and had an exaggerated view of their social standing. Angelina would soon have a full computer background check, but as she, and now I, suspected, impoverished gentry she was. Many people rich in past generations had dissipated family money for one reason or another, but held firm to their exalted notions of their worth to society. As she talked, I could hear inflections and affectations of a vaguely English accent. So, on with the interview.

"Mr. Stern, you came recommended as a fine barrister and so I've come for representation in a matter involving my son. I expect it will be somewhat large and time consuming."

"Alright, Mrs. Witherspoon, let me get a few facts here so I can see what we are talking about." I got out the yellow pad. "Let me have some basic information first. What is your name and address?"

"Mr. Stern, call me Whippy. It's much easier. Let me tell you about Avery first." "OK, what about Avery?"

"Avery's my son. We call him Andy. He was shot and in the hospital now under arrest.

Can you get him out?"

"What is he charged with?"

"Something to do with drugs, guns and a shooting." "So you want me to represent him in a criminal matter." "Yes. They said you were good."

"Do you know what happened that got him arrested?"

"Not too much. He told me over the phone to get him a lawyer and said he's been shot, and something about a drug deal."

"So tell me about Avery."

"Andy, he was a very nice boy. Good manners. Went to Locust Dale Academy like . . . oh . . . maybe three generations before him. They gave him a scholarship because the family had a legacy at the school." I looked at Angelina, who gave me a hefty eye roll. Yes. They were impoverished gentry but still had some clout in the WASP world. "He was a decent student, played soccer. And got into Trinity. His grades weren't quite good enough, but they seemed to like him." Another old boy perk. "But he left about mid-freshman year. He felt he was better as a musician."

"Did he play an instrument?"

"He was a disc jockey and said he had a knack for discovering talent."

"Any big names?"

"Not yet. But I've heard them. They're kind of folk-rock." "That era seems to have passed."

"You should hear his people. They can bring it back."

"So what does he do now?"

"He's mostly a DJ."

"Mr. Stern, I don't have much money, but I've been given some money for a retainer." She reached into a battered, but fine, leather handbag and took out an envelope with bills in it and pushed it across my desk.

"I'll have my paralegal give you a receipt." Angelina had just come in with a sheaf of printouts. "Angelina has already done some research on your son's case. Let me review it briefly. Could you give her some of your details and contact information."

"Surely," she turned to Angelina and I scanned what the internet had yielded. Mrs. Witherspoon's husband had two DUI's and there was a divorce matter pending for the past five years. He had a temporary alimony order out for $400 a week. Her son, Avery, had two prior arrests for minor drugs, both handled in "drug court" meaning they were minor matters and both were dismissed. Mrs. Witherspoon did not have anything significant, but she had gotten a small unemployment compensation award several years ago. She lived in a small apartment in the commercial section of the Main Line – a wealthy area in the Philadelphia suburbs.

"Uh-uh. Is he married?"

"No, he lives with a girl . . . well, sometimes. When they fight, he comes back and stays with me. Then, I guess they make up."

"So, how about his father."

"You mean Witless Witherspoon, the town drunk. No, he doesn't have much to do with Andy. His father worked for his family business which, when we got married, was doing well. They made Whitt kind of a salesman, customer man. He took their business customers out for a good time. In his day, he was a handsome fellow. I fell for it. When they sold the company, Whitt was bounced. He has some money tied up in a trust fund, but just enough income to live on. He works some and pays me alimony, but not much."

"So what about you?"

"I do crafts. I work part-time at an art store on "the Hill" and teach needlepoint." "So how did Andy get into such trouble?"

"I don't know. He DJ's around. He's in and out of rehab."

"Drugs?"

"I wouldn't say that, more depression. He's very sensitive." One of many massive eye rolls from Angelina.

"So, you really know nothing about the circumstances of his arrest?"

"No, only what he told me on the phone."

"How did you get this money for a retainer?"

"Some black person came to my apartment. Told me Andy was arrested and shot. He gave me this envelope and told me to get him a lawyer. I didn't know any lawyers. So they told me to get him a Jewish one. The people in my area knew you from

Locust Dale. So, here I am. Can you help my Andy?"

"I guess first I'll have to see him in the hospital. Where is he?"

"Presbyterian."

"Ok Mrs. Witherspoon, I'll take it from here. I'll stop by the hospital and interview your son today. They will probably have a bedside arraignment to set his bail. Since I don't really know the circumstances of his arrest, I can't say if he'll get low enough bail to go home, but at least I'll know what they are charging him with." Angelina escorted Mrs. Witherspoon out while I looked over Angelina's online information. There was a late news article that said he was found face down on a sidewalk in Powelton Village, just off the Penn campus. He was unconscious and shot in the shoulder.

Angelina came back. "So, Peter, you got a spoiled brat on your hands. Raised as a trust funder."

"Yeah, probably. Open a file. I'm going to get Carmen to see him in the hospital, maybe check out the scene where he was found."

I didn't have to look far for Carmen. She had been hanging just outside the door. She could smell action.

Carmen had been a client a few years before. She had been arrested on a prostitution charge, but together we not only beat it but parlayed the whole thing into a private boarding school in witness protection and a college education at LaSalle. She was now a paralegal in the office, but I could tell she was bored with the paperwork. She was at her best out on the streets doing investigation.

"I'm ready, Mr. Stern. Can we go now?"

Carmen was tough to rein in when she had a scent. So, yes, we could go now.

Presbyterian

ather than get a cab, Carmen and I took the subway up to
the Penn Campus and walked a few blocks to Presbyterian
Hospital, where the police controlled a wing for injured people
under arrest. After going through the metal detector and having
our bags searched, we were admitted and directed to Avery
Witherspoon's temporary residence – a hospital room with a
cell room door. A few guards kept watch in the hallway.

Avery shared the room with another wounded prisoner – a
young black kid with a heavy bandage around his neck. So, no
privacy.

"Avery, I'm Peter Stern. Your mother gave me a retainer to
represent you. This is Carmen Jacinto, my paralegal."

Avery sat up. "Whoa, she looks barely legal. She can sit over
here."

I shrugged my shoulders. Yes, Carmen was a looker. Petite
and even dressed in law office professional, she had a cute little
figure, but her dark eyes and wavy black shoulder length hair
sent out vibes that made men weak in the knees.

"So Avery, what are you charged with?"

"Something about drugs, guns and a shooting."

"Have you been told when you will be able to leave the
hospital?"

"They patched up my shoulder." He pointed to a heavy
bandage which ran up his right arm and round his shoulder. "It
was a through and through, so it just got soft tissue." He did speak
well and actually sounded as if he knew what he was talking

about. He had a Main Line, society accent – sort of affected fake British.   He was in his mid-thirties with long unkempt blond hair, a few days of blondish beard, and a handsome face.

The black kid on the other side of the curtain poked his head around the curtain. "So, Andy, you want I should go so you can talk."

"Yeah, Tariq. That would be great. Thanks." Tariq left and went out into the hallway. "So what happened?"

"I had just finished a DJ job at a rave on Lancaster Avenue and was going in my car when a car forced me to the side of the street, up by the curb. They got out, one guy had a gun, he was at my passenger side, yelling through the open window. Another guy was pulling at my door. They said, "Get the fuck out and give us your stuff." I guess I froze for a while, when the guy shot me in the shoulder. As I grabbed my right arm, the other guy pulled me out and threw me to the sidewalk. He had a gun on me. 'Don't move, motherfucker.' I didn't move. The guy who shot me was rummaging through the car.   I raised myself up on my good arm and the guy hit me with his pistol. That's all I remember. A little while later, a paddy wagon had pulled up and some cops brought me here."

"Did the cops find any drugs in your car?"

"Not that I know of."

"Did you have any in the car that night?"

"No."

"Did the cops put plastic bags on your hands?"

"I don't remember."

"Did you shoot anyone?"

"No."

"So why are they charging you?"

"Just preliminary I guess. They'll probably exonerate me later."

"I don't think so. What I hear is that you had drugs and a gun and maybe shot someone."

"Who told you that?"

"What you're charged with."

"Can't be."

OK, now it was time for the mantra defense lawyers repeat to their clients: First, I am on your side. If you don't tell me the truth and all the facts you know, I can't help you. If you are trying version no. 1 on me to see if it works, we will lose at trial because the police and the prosecutor are smarter than you. Second, there may be some facts that will help you. If I don't know them, they are worthless. Third, I then launched into the explanation about how to save yourself some significant jail time, if you have valuable information that the police can use, i.e. he who rats first, rats best. As usual this little dissertation drew the shocked and angry response that came from those who think they alone can beat the system.

"You mean you don't believe me?   How can I have a lawyer who doesn't trust me? What am I paying you for? Are you saying I'm gonna get jail time when I didn't do anything?" This rant went on for a while. I nodded to Carmen.

When he calmed down, I said, "Look, I'm just giving you the standard advice 1.0.   I don't know you yet. I haven't read the police reports. I am a lawyer. I always listen to all sides and do my own investigation. Yes. Sometimes, innocent people get convicted on bad evidence.

From what you tell me, the police should never have

arrested you. But I hear a few things that don't gibe. First, the police bagged your hands before taking you to the hospital. It says on your hospital notes. That means they are testing you for gunpowder residue. They didn't do it so that you wouldn't play with yourself in the paddy wagon. So it means there was a shooting and they think you did it. If you test positive for GPR, gun powder residue as they call it, you did some shooting. So I think they know more than I do. That's bad. So look, think things over. I've been a criminal defense lawyer and a prosecutor. I know more about the system than you do. Let me do my job. At this point, I do not believe or disbelieve anyone. I do my own investigation. If you don't like that, I'll walk and return the retainer."

He looked shocked. He wasn't prepared for someone he was paying to be disrespectful or even refuse his money. Somehow, he viewed me as being from a servant class and he was a lord of the manor.

"Well, I . . ."

"OK, now who paid me this retainer?"

"I don't know. Mom doesn't have that kind of money."

"Your girlfriend?"

"No way."

"This is important. Someone wants you to get a lawyer who won't rat them out. They want you to think you are being protected. That means that they expected you to get a lawyer who is among those connected to a drug ring. If you rat them out on a lawyer's advice, the lawyer doesn't get any more business from the drug ring. Got it! The lawyer really represents the ring because he is paid by the ring."

"I didn't . . ."

"No, you didn't. That is what I'm here for. I do. I'm not a run of the mill criminal defense attorney. I usually do civil cases. That means I'm not in this club, so I don't rely on drug rings sending me clients. Your mom got lucky, I'm independent."

"She says you're Jewish."

"True."

"She says they're the best."

"I like to think so. It's good for business. But there are all kinds. Anyway, I'll work with you if you work with me. Don't tell me any more stories until I hear what the police reports say. Then I'll have more questions. Ok?"

"Yeah, good."

"Let me know when they schedule your arraignment. I'll be over. They'll set your bail then and I'll find out more about their case against you. Ok?"

"Yeah, good." Carmen and I went back to the subway.

"So Carmen, what do you think?"

"First, he's a pretty boy, spoiled by his mom who wasn't too happy with dad."

"So far so good."

"He has half a brain hidden in there somewhere, but thinks he knows more than he does." "I'll go along with that."

"He's in the drug scene. Those DJ's always are. He's a small time dealer in stuff college kids take. He thinks he's cool and knows the whole scene, but he's small potatoes. They'll dump him if he gets dangerous." Carmen was well aware of the practice that the big dealers will often sell out one of their own dealers to garner credit with the DEA or local cops who can then pad their stats. Our Avery was an obvious choice to be dumped when necessary. He was small time and he was not connected to anyone with power, but he was at least worth $5,000 to protect and he had at least $5,000 worth of dirt on the big boys.

"Good call, Carmen."

"That's nothing, Pete. I'm just warming up. Yes there was a shooting. He shot someone, maybe killed him. So he's big enough to carry, but he didn't know how or when to use it. So he got shot and probably robbed."

"By who?"

"A rival drug gang or just some freelancers who knew he was dealing. He was vulnerable. He was a DJ, meaning a visible drug dealer. He had the night's stash in Powelton Village so he's an easy target."

"Probably, all right."

"And then, he's so stupid that he tries a dumb story on a lawyer, and gets mad when you tell him he might walk or get a light sentence if he rats his source or the robbers out. I think he can do both."

"Carmen, you are a gem. First thing we have to do is see who will threaten him if he rats them out. I don't think they will do it at the hospital, but someone in the slammer will. That will be interesting. I also think his mom may be threatened. She's somewhat alcoholic and may do something strange. We'll have to talk to her."

While we were standing on the subway platform, I got a call from Angelina. The judge and the district attorney were on their way to the hospital to arraign Avery. So, no need to go back to the office and return later. We went back to the hospital detention wing. As we got there, the judge, et al were setting up in Avery's room for a bail hearing. A public defender had come along to represent Avery in case he had no lawyer. I notified everyone of my representation and filled out an Entry of Appearance form. Meanwhile, court personnel were taking down personal information from Avery used in determining bail. A number of factors were used: the seriousness of the alleged crime, the defendant's ties to the community, i.e. where he lived, where he worked and for how long, family connections, etc.

As we all assembled at bedside, the court officer read out their findings. Avery was charged with an amount of different drugs to exceed the maximum level for the "drug court," a tribunal for minor drug cases. He was also charged with possession of a gun and attempted murder. Certainly not what he told me earlier. There was no further information on that now. He had said he lived with his mother, he had said for the last five years (that did not square with what he said about his girl friend). He said he had a regular job as a DJ and was not on welfare. He had no children. Under the new rules making it easier to get bail, even though he was charged with some serious crimes, bail was set at $100,000. Under the system, he could get out by posting just $10,000. If he showed for all court appearances, he would get $7,000 back at the end of the matter. So, not too bad. Avery got a call from someone who said they were posting bail. I asked him who this someone was, but he said he couldn't say. But now he would be out as soon as the doctors at the hospital released him. I handed him some of my cards as he continued to ogle Carmen. I explained that we would soon have a preliminary hearing at which we would find out what this case was all about. 'Til then, I still had no idea why he had been arrested. So, as Carmen and I turned to leave, Avery asked for "a few bucks." He had no money on him and wanted train fare to his mother's. I gave him $10.

It was still just early afternoon so Carmen and I decided to look at the site where Avery was found. It was just outside the Powelton Village area in Mantua, so we walked. It was a simple block of old West Philadelphia row houses along 3900 Apple Street. We walked up and down around the middle of the block while the neighbors came out to gawk at a guy in a suit walking up and down with a petite young Latina in a short skirt and blouse. We made a few attempts at talking to the neighbors about the incident where the police picked up a white guy on their sidewalk. We got no answers. None. So Carmen took a number of photos of the site and we walked back to the subway. There were several sites with what looked like blood spatter. She took pictures and noted the addresses where the blood was found. But Carmen had seen a nice restaurant just off the Penn Campus. Her appetite, as always, is prodigious so I was persuaded to have lunch there at my treat. The menu was mostly Italian, so Carmen ordered chicken parm, Caesar salad and a large raspberry banana smoothie. To balance things out, and because tomorrow was my day at the gym, I had a salad with shrimp and Italian dressing and an iced green tea.

"Something hinky about the site," Carmen said while wolfing down large bites of chicken parm with a side of pasta. "No one knows or will say anything. Something is going on there."

"I agree. We should talk to the cops who picked Avery up." Carmen, who like small birds seemed to consume twice her body weight each meal, ordered a tortufo for desert on my tab. This wonderful Italian delicacy has two kinds of ice cream covered in dark chocolate. I decided to let the firm cover this bill and pulled out the firm charge card. If I had had what Carmen had for lunch, I would have needed a nap, but she was chattering away about her thoughts as we hopped on the subway back to the office.

First Preliminary Hearing

The preliminary hearing was scheduled for this morning, so Carmen and I went over to the Criminal Justice Center. This building built on a side street in center city was a monument to poor design. From 9:00 a.m. to 10:00 a.m. there was an enormous crush of people into the small lobby which housed two metal detectors for those destined for 100 courtrooms trying criminal cases. You certainly couldn't argue with metal detectors for those involved in criminal cases, but at some point it had to dawn on those in line that about half of the people they were pressed up against were accused of some felony, mostly violent in nature. Fortunately, lawyers had lobbied early to be let through by showing a Bar I.D. card, but Carmen had to go through the jam with the rest of the peons. I went to the courtroom reserved for homicide cases and registered my appearance for Avery. For some arcane reason, newspapers were not permitted in the courtrooms. This arose out of the precaution that the news might have some reference to the case which might spoil the jury pool. Since this room never held jury trials, there was no reason to exclude newspapers. I was usually admonished for secretively doing the day's Suduko. So, I went out to the hallway and took out the Philadelphia Inquirer. Soon, Carmen came up and took out her paper as well, the Al Dia, the Latino newspaper.

All people were put on notice to show up at 9:00 a.m. which really meant 9:30. Nonetheless, Avery sauntered in at 10:00 a.m. I had forgotten to tell him how to dress for trial – like someone the judge and jury might not mind seeing walking the streets late at night. But really, they should look like their lives would be wasted behind bars. Avery, however, was wearing a black t-shirt from some obscure heavy metal band on tour with fire and some satanic symbols. He was unshaven and he looked like he just rolled out of bed. He greeted us dimly. "Yo, hullo." Since this was just a preliminary hearing, and he was not appearing to be too coherent, now was not the time for one of the several defense lawyer lectures. After all, he would not testify today. The prosecutor only had to put on enough evidence to convince the judge that there was sufficient evidence for the matter to go on to a formal trial. This would be scheduled for a conference and a trial date after the proceedings today. So Avery sat next to Carmen and stared dully forward. Poor Carmen was subjected to a heavy aroma of body odor, tobacco breath and an invasion of personal space as he nestled closer to my little Latina paralegal.

Since it was now past 10:00 a.m., I thought I should go into the courtroom to see how the list of cases was progressing. We were no. 4 on a list of 9 that day. The court clerk, a political appointee and thus unfireable, had gone to rude school so she felt it was time to put down a few lawyers. Of course, some regular defense lawyers courted her and bought her drinks at their after hours hang out, but I was not a regular and so not entitled to a shred of courtesy. As I stood at the bar of court patiently waiting for her to acknowledge my presence while she chatted with the police liaison women to her left, she finally turned and barked.

"What!"

"I'm number 4 on the list. How does it look today?"

"The judge is not in yet, nor are the cops, so cool your heels counselor."

"I'll be in the hall if I'm needed."

"Got it, 4, I'll let you know." She said over her shoulder as she turned to the liaison lady.

Lawyers in the county courts are usually subjected to abuse – probably because the clerks now have the opportunity to put down someone. The court personnel reflect what lawyers call "the black robe disease." Judges in Pennsylvania and most places are products of the electoral system. So a few committeemen are cobbled together by a lot of donations from the candidate or the political faithful to put a lawyer with mediocre qualifications on the bench and in charge of our liberties. These judges are yanked from the nether regions of the bar and elevated to preside over lawyers who can actually earn a living practicing law. As a result, they get the opportunity to abuse and disconcert those appearing before them. The clerks imitate their attitudes.

I went back outside in the hallway. Avery was talking to some woman in a heated conversation. I sat by Carmen and finished the hard Suduko for the day. By 10:30, I went back in again and avoided the clerk and spoke to one of my fellow defense lawyers.

"So, how are we doing?" "The judge isn't in yet." "But it's 10:30."

"Yeah, well, this is Judge Carson." "So do they dock his pay."

"Yeah, as if."

I went back outside. Avery was still gesturing wildly at some woman with her back to us. Probably his girl friend, nice figure, faded jeans, good butt, and a jean jacket. Carmen broke out some of her snacks and was munching on some trail mix.

By 11:00 a.m. the police liaison lady came out, "Mr. Stern?" "That's me."

"Well, it turns out that the shooting victim is not dead, but in Presbyterian Hospital. We were just told. So the case is not a homicide, just an attempted murder and aggravated assault. So you're not in homicide court anymore. We'll reschedule you for later."

"Can you let me know now?"

"Don't think so. We'll send you a notice."

My shoulders slumped. Two billable hours wasted. Carmen went to tell Avery and I texted to Angelina. So we started back to the office.

We passed the door to the room where the cops awaited their call to testify. Carmen held me back. "Wait, Pete, maybe we can talk to the officers at the scene." Sure enough, Perez and Williams came out the door.

Carmen had now dressed for the part. She was wearing a short skirt and loose silk blouse. I hadn't noticed before, but she must have put on a push-up bra. Normally petite, she had become, shall I say, voluptuous. I now noticed the eye makeup complete with liner and lashes. She was in character. I didn't need to be told twice. I took Williams aside and asked him a few questions in a straightforward manner. Carmen had now cornered poor Officer Perez.

I held on to Williams as long as I could, but he looked over at Perez and saw he was in pickup mode.

"So, Julio, I'll see you back at the station." Perez didn't reply, just waved. I sat on the bench and did the middle and hard Suduko in the free handout paper. I could see Carmen had had her tablet out and was showing Officer Perez some video. He was nodding. So she must have gotten something. I saw him write down something and leave. Carmen strutted over to me.

"Got something?"

"Yeah, Pete, piece of cake. He knows my uncle from San Juan."

"Oh yeah. And he got your phone number."

"Well, that too."

"Are you going to bill the firm for your wardrobe enhancements and makeup?"

"You bet. He says He'll help me but to contact him later."

Avery Back in Office

I had asked Avery to come into the office for a conference based on the new information we now had on his case. While scheduled for 10:00 a.m., a decent time for late sleepers, he ambled in about noon. It seemed he had at least showered and combed his hair. He was definitely handsome, a good factor in front of a jury. We certainly would need all women. He had on another black t-shirt with a long forgotten hard rock band and a scuffed up, but fashionable, leather jacket. We could see some very expensive tattoos on his arms – a few Asian letters, a skull, probably a parrot and some florals. From my previous knowledge, I guess we were looking at at least $5,000 and maybe $10,000 worth of ink on a guy who was not a big earner. I was guessing now that he did well pushing drugs at his DJ gigs. Carmen, who had been learning her eye roll technique from Angelina was clearly not impressed.

"So, Avery. We have a lot more information than we did before. You didn't tell us much before and that makes my job harder. The harder for me, the worse for you. It seems you were involved in a shootout with your drug dealer at somewhere on Apple Street at about 2:00 a.m. Do you want to tell us about it?"

"I was? I was unconscious and the next thing I remember was waking up in the hospital. It's all a blur." I couldn't figure out why Avery was not forthcoming. It must be that he was playing for time and hoping something good might happen.

"It seems you showed up at 2:00 and yelled at someone on Apple Street. Do you know what number on Apple? You pulled out a gun (which probably will be identified as the shooter) and threatened this guy and were winged by a shooter out the second floor window. You shot the guy on the first floor. It seems he hit you with something and you went down. Does this ring a bell?" I had gotten this from Carmen's notes from her talk with Officer Perez.

He bent his head down and was shaking it. "No, no, that's all made up. Someone's playing me."

"Do you own a hand gun?" "No."

"Do you get drugs from Apple Street for resale at your raves?"

"No. I don't touch that stuff." He rubbed his nose. Carmen gave a major eye roll. "So, that didn't happen?"

"Not that I remember."

"Nice. Look, Avery . . ." "Andy."

"Ok, Andy. They put plastic bags on your hands for a reason. They are looking for gun powder residue. If it's on your hands, you were a shooter. If they bagged your hands, that means they found your brass."

"My brass?"

"Yeah, the shell casings from a weapon. They can identify the gun from the marks on the shell casings. Once they put the gun on you, they can match the bullet back to you. Someone in Apple Street was shot. At first they told us he died, but it looks like he's still living. So that means they dug the bullet out of him. Would that be your bullet?"

"Dunno."

"They also found a gun on the sidewalk. Will it match the brass and the bullet in the guy at Apple Street?"

"Look, I think this is all a set up. I gotta tell you they took my cell phone. Can they do that?"

"They what? Andy, they may be able to find God-knows-what on there. Can you remember what's on there?"

He looked puzzled. "Don't they need a search warrant for that?"

"So now you're a constitutional scholar? What's on there?" "Could be lots of stuff."

"Like drug deals?"

"No, can't be." Another Carmen eye roll.

"Look, Andy, you could be in big trouble. Drugs, guns and attempted murder. You have got to get a better memory. It doesn't look good so far."

"No, well they got a search warrant for my mom's apartment. They got nothing."

"How about your girlfriend's place?"

"They don't know about that yet."

"Was she the one we saw with you at the Criminal Justice Center?"

"Yeah. What of it?"

"Are you married to her?" "No way."

"She can be a witness then. There is no spousal immunity. What does she know if they call her?"

"Nothing. There's nothing to know."

"Look, Andy. You are looking at some serious prison time. I'm guessing 20 to 30 years. We've been paid to help you out. We don't know by whom. We have some ideas. But, frankly, I don't think you are being straight with us. I have to say the police version could sound plausible to a jury."

"So do the best you can. I'm getting help elsewhere."

"That sounds ominous. When you get in bed with these drug

organizations, they are not nice people. You are small potatoes to them. You are expendable. They'll turn on you in a second.

"Yeah, yeah, yeah. I'll take my chances."

"Look, I also have to tell you as your attorney, they don't want you as much as they want them. If you cooperate with the District Attorney, I could save you lots of time in the slammer and I could get you prime facilities. Otherwise, you are in with the scum in some godawful upstate prison."

"I hear you. Look. Just do your job."

"I've said what I had to say. The preliminary hearing has been rescheduled for next Thursday. Try to look presentable. That goes a long way. Shave, nice clothes, hair combed."

"Yeah, yeah. See you next Thursday."

Preliminary Hearing

The rescheduled Preliminary Hearing date had arrived. As before, I squeezed through the massive collection of humanity bunched into the poorly designed lobby in front of the metal detectors. I observed once again that about half of this horde were convicted felons or accused perpetrators. I took the elevator to the sixth floor crushed in a melange of police, perps, witnesses and lawyers. I checked in at the courtroom and shook hands with the Assistant District Attorney and was vastly relieved.

Some prosecutors withhold evidence until the last possible moment in hopes that the defense attorney will be unable to prepare his case or locate defense witnesses. Others believe in full and fair disclosure. After all, prosecutors have the benefit of all manner of experts – ballistic, fingerprint, drug analysis, etc. and the full complement of police power at their fingertips. The defendant usually lacks funds and can only hope his attorney can pick apart the prosecutor's evidence. But today, I had Malcolm Aspin for the hearing. He was a full disclosure guy and had a file of discovery materials for me. I sat in the back row and thumbed through the neatly assembled and copied files and hoped my client would show up on time. As I had guessed, the evidence against Avery was mounting up and could be overwhelming. Another reason, Malcolm was so accommodating. He expected a guilty plea and probable cooperation against his drug sources. This was always better than a trial lasting a week.

As expected, there was the IBIS report. The government maintains files of ballistic records just like fingerprints. The firing of a gun leaves a series of scoring marks on the lead of the bullet head, this much TV had made clear. But most bullets lodge inside bodies, or are too distorted to provide a provable match to a gun. Little known, however, is the mark by the firing pin on the brass shell casing. So if "brass" from the gun is left at the scene of the shooting, it can be matched certifiably to the weapon. That was the case here for our Avery. The revolver found near his outstretched hand, a Taurus Raging Bull .44 magnum. Not exactly a Saturday night special, but on the cheaper end, but with maximum damage potential. This gun was somewhat rare, but was easily matched to its shell casings. Not good for Avery.

The bullet was still inside the alleged victim who lay in the Presbyterian Hospital criminal detention wing recovering from his wounds. Maybe they could extract the bullet, maybe not.

There was now a drug report. It seems they had gotten a search warrant for the car Avery had been driving. It was registered to an Aliyah Rosen. In the well covered by the spare tire in the trunk, there was a smorgasbord of drugs: coke, ecstacy, meth and a few designers, all neatly bagged. They had been dusted for fingerprints, but none were found. They were all stamped with the brand of a bulldog, a familiar brand from a west Philly source usually found east of Market Street on up to City Line and east to the railroad line. Avery's cooperation could aid in bringing down this drug distribution gang on Apple Street and a major part of west Philly.

The police report detailed the interview of Ms. Jackson from 3939 Apple Street who witnessed the argument and shooting from her second floor bedroom window, about fifty feet from where the shooting occurred. Avery had drawn his gun and aimed it at the man in the doorway who was later found shot, when a rifle was pointed out the second floor and fired at Avery, hitting his right shoulder. This mountain of evidence was not looking good for Avery.

About then, Avery sauntered in and signed in with the court clerk. He had at least listened to me about his appearance. He had shaved, his hair was cut, and he wore a fashionable tweed jacket and a blue button down shirt and khakis. He was almost preppy. I waived to him to go out in the hall. He nodded. So, we sat on the benches in the hallway. When I checked in again with the court clerk, I heard some cases from another courtroom had been dumped in our room. It was already looking like we would not get on before lunchtime and now we would not be heard until in the afternoon.

I took Avery into a small conference room off the court. "Andy, it looks bad. The ballistic results are from a gun found next to you on the sidewalk."

"But I heard the bullet is still in the other guy." I wondered how he knew that. He was obviously getting help elsewhere.

"That is true so far, but they can match the shell casing to the firing pin and the model of the gun – the one found next to you."

"Someone's framing me."

"You had gun powder residue on your hands." I said flipping another piece of the prosecutor's discovery file.

"So it was self-defense." A completely different defense.

"Do you remember how it happened. You may have to testify if we claim self-defense." "I can't remember now." The 'now' was a bit suspicious. He was trying to craft a plausible defense, but only after the evidence was in.

"Can you give me at least the address of the shooting scene?"

"Dunno."

"Well, we'll hear the eyewitness today. She'll say you started having an argument with someone in the house and drew your gun. Someone at the second floor window winged you and you fired back three times."

"What does she know! An old lady from down the street." (I hadn't told him that.) "What could she see?"

I shrugged. "Look, Andy, if you let me in on what you know, I can possibly help you. Don't try to be a lawyer. Just give me the facts and let me do my job." Again the shrug. "They also got a search warrant for the car you were driving. They found a variety of drugs in the spare tire wheel well."

"It's not my car."

"No. It seems it's registered to an Aliyah Rosen who lives in Fishtown. Didn't you tell me you lived at this address?"

"Yeah. That's my girlfriend. It's her car."

"So she could be charged with possession too. At this point, you're looking at attempted murder, attempted robbery, gun violations, drug possession and a few others. So far, I add this up on the guidelines to about 35 years. This is serious. I need your help."

"So what if I did all these things and I rat out some people."

"Good question. It depends on who you give up and how good your evidence is. I'd say at least the sentence could go down to about 5 or 10 years. And most importantly, you go to a minimum security prison, maybe Allenwood. That's not hard time."

"Nah. I'd get killed."

"That depends. I could get you maximum segregation. You wouldn't be anywhere near those people."

"Nah. I'm good." This time it was for me to shrug.

"Ok. Our case won't come up for a while. Maybe late afternoon. So go back to the courtroom." We both left the small conference room. A woman was sitting in the hallway. She got up and started yelling at Avery.

"Andy, you stupid shmuck." Her tirade went on.

It was not hard to figure out that this was Andy's girlfriend, Aliyah Rosen, the owner of the impounded car. The woman was dressed in a peasant skirt and an embroidered jean jacket. From what I could see, she was slim. As Andy turned to face her, I was shocked to discover she was my former fiancée of fifteen years ago, Alison Rosen. As her tirade went on, I recalled back all those years.

She had been a very sexy hippie then in the Museum School of Art while I was in law school. Her world was artsy. I have to say this irritated me. When the under-educated are given the artistic freedom of the bohemian class, they say and do some really dumb things. At the art school parties, everyone was high, at least on grass, and in between snatches of popular music, they would say 'Wow, this is good shit!' The mood was easy and loose and the girls were easy, as was Alison. She genuinely enjoyed sex and thought, or at least I believed she thought, I was the greatest thing in the world. How we got engaged, I'll never know.

After law school, I knew I'd be drafted, so I signed on for officer training for three years instead of the two as an enlisted man. I continued to see Alison when I would return home on leave. I guess I was lonely, or worn out from the mind-numbing military training. Somehow, I was persuaded that getting engaged would be a good thing, so I did. An excellent test of a relationship. I discovered her world and her friends were irritatingly self-absorbed and uneducated. I discovered that she did not fit in my world. But most of that was hindsight. My friends were educated, aware of current issues, had read widely. She was more interested in fashion, but mainly herself.

Soon, I had to be gone on a long training session. She came down once and was disgusted by the military camp. Not long after that, she said she wanted to date other people and she did. Being deserted while you are stuck in the military is not only unpleasant, but a major blow to your ego. So she left. I got through my military assignment, most boring and wasteful of my time, and went on to become a lawyer. I harbored considerable resentment against Alison for deserting me when I was down, but over the years, this had dissipated. The best revenge is living well.

After reliving in my head some of the scenes from our past relationship, I tuned back in to the tirade in the hallway next to me.

It seems the police had traced the car at the shooting scene to Alison and gotten her address off the registration. Since there were a vast supply of drugs in the wheel well in the trunk, the cops got a search warrant for her apartment, which they executed at 6:00 a.m. The cops love those early morning intrusions. Gotta love 'em. She was still half asleep in her nightie as they handed her the warrant and proceeded to toss the apartment looking for drugs or weapons. They found none.

Apparently, Alison, now Aliyah, was not aware of Avery/Andy's extensive drug dealing and, since she was paying the rent, was angry that he had exposed her to this humiliation. Later, she discovered that her car, a gift from her father, had been impounded since it had been used in the commission of a crime.

However, since she was now aware that her Avery/Andy was a drug dealer, she decided to search the apartment more thoroughly and in places the cops had not. She found wads of 10's and 20's neatly wrapped in rubber bands stashed behind the kitchen sink. This particularly irritated her because she had been paying for more than her share of their living expenses.

The tirade was apparently far from over when I raised my hand to intervene. She was, after all, spouting valuable pieces of information the prosecution could use. Fortunately, the hallway was filled with many other women berating their men, who were now criminal defendants, for a variety of shortcomings.

She turned to me as I was shushing her. "Oh, hello, Peter. Nice to see you after all these years." Her voice had lowered several registers and was all sweetness now. "You know I told his mother to hire you. You were always a straight arrow and would give him an honest representation."

"Uh, hullo, is it Aliyah now?"

"Yes. I've gotten more spiritual." I was not going to comment on her spirituality as defined by her choice of boyfriend. I made the mistake, however, of glancing at Avery/Andy as she was saying this.

She barked, "Oh sure, rub it in. You vindinctive MF."

"Whoa, easy now. I . . ." As usual my efforts to cool the situation, especially here in the hallway were ignored. I was lucky that Avery/Andy had taken a breath as if to speak, and he was drowned in the tirade now directed at him. I sat on the nearby bench and began to thumb through the file the ADA had given me. I had to smirk inwardly at the awful choice Alison, now Aliyah, had made. As I could hear the tirade beginning to subside, I asked them both to step inside a small conference room. I told the court clerk where I would be and met them in the room.

"Look, Alison, I don't know if you're paying for me or not."

"Not. I can't afford you." (Ah, two points for the good guy.) "You and your Armani suit." (Actually, it was a closeout from Syms).

"Well, I've been thinking that that is important. I'll explain later. I'll also explain how you might be able to get your car back. I say 'might'. It is not assured. And I also have to explain that you might be arrested for possession yourself."

"What! What!" She turned and started to hone in with a laser stare at Andy.

"Hold on! Hear me out. This is important." I then went into a recital of all the evidence compiled against Andy and how it did not look good. I looked at Andy who gave me a shrug and a dumb smirk. "I haven't heard Andy's side of the story yet."

"What, you shmuck. You have a real lawyer here and you don't use him." I had to shush her again.

"Look, you two, I think I can figure what is going on. I was paid by Andy's drug source because they don't want him to cooperate with the Assistant District Attorney and rat out their organization. If he is convicted, he would be looking at at least 15 to maybe 25 years. I don't think Aliyah (the name stuck in my throat) will wait for you to get out." (Another inward smirk.)

"I'm sure he'll have lots of anal sex in jail." Alison/Aliyah blurted.

"Calm down and listen. If he cooperates, he may get three or four years, maybe less depending on the value of his information. The cops and the DA know me as a straight shooter, so they'll be willing to make me a good deal."

"No way." Andy shrugged.

"But, and here is a big but, the drug gang will not want to hear you're cooperating and may harm you. They may also focus on Aliyah or even your mom. Maybe even me."

"Wonderful, just wonderful. You shmuck!" She said. Andy was lower than whale shit now.

"Look, Aliyah, so far they haven't done anything to you yet and they may not. But they could also try to squeeze Andy by arresting you and charging you with joint possession. Of course, that case would not stand up in court. But they may want Andy to cooperate and as part of the deal and let you off. You will have some trouble reclaiming your car."

A possibly more intense laser stare from Alison/Aliyah.

"So today, we'll have a preliminary hearing. I'll at least hear the eyewitness testimony. I'll have to waive the expert witness testimony – drug lab, gun powder residue, blood tests. It's usually done for preliminary hearings. I may find some holes in the eyewitness' account. Let's see. Then, I'll talk to Andy again. So, where will I be able to reach you?"

"At my moms."

"Good, the less the cops can trace Aliyah to the drugs, the better for her."

We went out and sat in the hallway outside the courtroom. A sullen silence prevailed. Avery/Andy sat staring at his hands. Alison/Aliyah paced. I sat and was making a to do a list of items back at the office. We were excused by the court clerk when the judge went out for lunch. I went to the Reading Terminal alone for lunch and told the two lovebirds to be back by 2:00. The Reading Terminal was a delightful mélange of eateries and book stalls. For a change, I had an oyster stew at a seafood counter and phoned the office. Angelina had nothing new, but she gave me a list of my phone calls.   I sorted through the list and called, in order, the important ones, the pleasant ones and saved the unpleasant ones for a happier time.

When I got back to the courtroom and checked in, the court clerk said we would be second in line and told me to sit in the room. I made sure Avery sat next to me.

The judge was a nice older black woman. For preliminary hearings, her job was easy. She had to decide if she had heard enough evidence that there would be a trial on the accusations the prosecutor made. Today, there was sure to be enough so I would have no quarrel with her on that score. The sole purpose today was to find out as much as I could about the evidence and prepare for the trial. I already had the expert reports – the gun powder residue, the shell casing match to the gun, the drug lab report, the search warrant for the car. There was no sense irritating the court by demanding evidence on those points, so I stipulated the written reports could go in as evidence without forcing the actual witnesses to come and testify. So, the only witnesses were the officers who found Avery at the scene and the lady from 3939 Apple Street who was an eyewitness to the argument and the shooting.

When our turn came, Officer Perez went first. He was straightforward and, in a near monotone, described receiving a call about a shooting victim on Apple Street. At 2:30 a.m., he and his partner went to the scene and found Avery unconscious on his back at 3929 with a bleeding wound to the right shoulder, and a blunt force wound to the right side of his head. He called an ambulance and Avery was transported to the hospital. A red, late model Audi A3 was still running near the scene with driver's door open in the lane where Avery lay. A vehicle license trace showed it belonged to Aliyah Rosen at a Fishtown residence which matched that on Avery's driver's license. A number of brass shell casings were retrieved from the scene and bagged. In addition, Avery's hands were encased in plastic bags to be tested later for gun powder residue. Apple Street was quiet and no one came out to the police cruiser or the ambulance. A forensic lady came on the scene and started to collect the physical evidence and take photos. A diagram of the street showed Avery's outline in front of 3927 Apple Street. The shell casings were on the sidewalk and street in front of 3918 Apple Street. The prosecutor, a pleasant but somewhat nerdy young lady led the officer through his story. I rapidly made notes and could find little to pick at. One fact stood out. Avery had been found on his back on the west side of the street, yet the shell casings were 50 feet away in front of the east side of Apple Street on the even number side of the street. I spent some time asking how Avery could have been found about fifty feet from where the shell casings were found. The gun found near him on the sidewalk was now fifty feet from the shell casings. How could that have happened?

Next, a police photographer came in with photos of the shooting victim from Presbyterian Hospital. He was Artemus Young, also known as "Pug Dog", a black male, 26 years of age and resided at Melon Street, around the block from the 3900 block of Apple Street. He had a bullet wound to his upper left chest, lower left leg and right thigh. He was now in stable condition. He would not be appearing for the hearing. I would not be able to cross examine him about the argument and the shooting. It was expected that he would refuse to testify anyway and would assert his Fifth Amendment rights. I so noted, but then how could they claim that Avery shot him?

That question was to be answered by Ms. Jackson. She was a nicely dressed middle-aged black woman and she testified that she lived at 3939 Apple Street and was asleep in the front bedroom of the second floor in the early morning hours. She heard some shouting and saw a white man had gotten out of his car and was hammering on the door on the other side of Apple Street. She was able to make out the words "short bags" in his shouts. Someone came to the door, a short stocky black man and began to shout back. The white man pulled a gun from inside the car and held it on the black man, but a second story window of the Apple Street house was slammed open and a rifle protruded out. A brief flash came out of the muzzle and the white man fell to the ground. He retrieved his gun off the pavement and fired several times at the black man. A second black man came out of the house with what looked like a baseball bat and hit the white man on the right side of the head. At that point, the second black man began to look around the neighborhood, so Ms. Jackson ducked back from her window and hid. She later heard a car pull up, stop and then drive off. Several minutes later, a police car pulled up with its lights flashing. At that point, feeling that things were safe again, she put on her bathrobe and came outside to ask the police what had happened. She gave a statement as to what she saw. The prosecutor then said, "No further questions."

I was scribbling furiously to get my notes straight as the judge asked, "Counsel?"

"Yes, your honor. Just a minute please as I checked off topics in my notes to pursue.

Then I looked up at Ms. Jackson.

"Ms. Jackson, do you live at 3939 Apple Street, across from where you saw the shooting?" I was now pointing at an enlarged city plot plan of the 3900 block of Apple Street.

"Yes."

"In front of which house was the white man standing?"

"I couldn't say. Several doors down, across the street, about 3916 or so."

"Do you know any of the houses on the other side of the street to be where drugs are sold?"

"No. I couldn't say." An obvious lie. She must be concealing the location out of fear of retaliation from the drug dealers.

"So you can't or won't say which house was the location of the shooting?"

At this point the prosecutor objected. "Your Honor, 'won't' implies she is withholding evidence."

I turned to the judge. "Your Honor, this is cross-examination. I asked if she is withholding. She may be committing a crime herself by obstructing justice." A not too subtle threat.

"The witness can answer."

"No, counsel, I can't say."

"Well, when you went out to meet the police, did you go down to the scene?"

"No, I was on my front stoop."

"So, where was the white man laying?"

"On my side of the street, about five doors down, maybe 3929."

"Was he on his stomach or back?"

"Back."

"Did you see the police photographing shell casings?"

"Yes. They were all further down the street from where the white man was laying."

"Where was the gun?"

"Near the white man's right hand."

"Do you known Artemus Young?" "No. Who's he?"

"The stocky black man who was shot."

"No."

I ended my cross-examination, made a few notes. Avery had been sitting next to me. I said, "Andy, don't say anything until we are outside. Then we can talk." He nodded. I led Andy/Avery and Alison/Aliyah out and down to the elevator. Once outside, I got the usual question. "How does it look?"

I shook my head. "Not so good. Andy, you've got to talk to me."

"But what about self-defense? I mean they shot first. I was just trying to get out of there."

"Self-defense doesn't work that way. I'll have to explain it in more detail back in the office. I have to think through a few things. Like you won't ever testify. Ms. Jackson buries you, but she has the location of the shooting and where your body was found all wrong. I have to think this through."

"Andy, listen to him, will you!" Aliyah was right, but I was sure Andy was getting his advice somewhere else. It was getting complicated, but I still thought Andy was cooked. They left. I think Andy went to Suburban Station to take the train to the suburbs and his mother, while Alison took the el down to Fishtown and her apartment. I went back to the office just as most of the people were leaving. Angelina and Carmen were waiting anxiously. They wanted a full report on the preliminary hearing. I went though most of it when Angelina said,

"What, whoa! She's your ex-fiancée from way back when." "Yeah, like 15 years ago."

"She dumped you while you were in the military.

I wasn't going to escape this cross-examination. So I explained. Angie always liked a soap opera. Carmen sat shocked that someone might reject me. But they had the whole story.

"So, Peter, were you angry?"

"Yeah. Sure, but that was way in the past."

"Watch yourself, Peter. I don't like the looks of this. Nor will Lynn."

My wife, Lynn, had already had the full story from the past. I was now happily married, two kids, a mortgage, a station wagon, the whole bit. Lynn was a high school teacher, very pretty and a fitness fanatic. Angelina and Carmen both knew Lynn and had a great time trading stories at my expense. Angelina was not about to let me get into trouble over this Aliyah.

"Pete, you have to tell your wife she's involved in this case."

"Yeah, yeah, I know." I did know. So I told her at dinner that night.

I listened as Angelina and Carmen picked at the case. It looked bleak, but Carmen wanted to take a look at the scene with me again. She called Officer Perez, who was only too happy to hear from her.

"So, Pete, Perez says he can help us. I'm sure he knows

something. Let's go tomorrow." "Sure thing. I'll bet you liked that Italian restaurant."

"Wouldn't miss it. On the firm too."

I sat in the small conference room with Carmen and Angelina in front of the city plot plan. Ms. Jackson's house was marked in green, Avery's body in black, the brass shell casings in yellow.

"Ladies, we are not getting the true picture. Avery's body had to be in front of the drug house, not several doors up the street and on the odd number side. It's that simple.

"Ms. Jackson must know where the drug house is on the even numbered side. Everyone on the block knows where the drug house is, but won't say."

"If Avery's body was moved from the drug house, the gun and the shell casings should be as well. There's something fishy here."

"Now, in Carmen's photos there are blood spots. A small amount where he was found at 3929, but more at 3926 and 3918. So, one must be the drug house or nearby, but why the second blood spot at 3926."

"In a criminal case, every discrepancy can cause reasonable doubt, so we need answers." "Peter, I think Perez will help us out tonight. I think that's what he meant. I suspect he and the other cops in the district know which is the drug house."

"I agree. That's an important missing piece. We certainly could not go to the probable drug house site and ask if there was a drug dispute and shooting in front of their house."

Now, how about the fact that he was later found unconscious on the opposite side of the street with the shell casings and gun nearby. There would be no explanation for this illogical twist to Ms. Jackson's testimony.

Sometimes, an irrelevant loose end can confuse a jury. As one of my brilliant law professors would say, it is the "thirteenth stroke of the clock." As he explained, "if you are lying in bed in the dark and you hear the church bell chime three times, you are inclined to think it is three o'clock in the morning. If you hear it chime thirteen times, you have no idea what time it is. So you make the argument to the jury that when they hear the proverbial thirteenth stroke of the clock, everything that went before it is false."

Fair enough. But I knew that the unconscious Avery could have been dragged to new locations to disguise the location of a drug house, but the judge and jury would never know that. I was now in possession of poisonous information. I could not breach a duty to my client and reveal it to anyone else. On the other hand, I had a duty not to assert a falsehood at trial. Yet, the missing information as to the strange location of the unconscious Avery was a loose end. For the time being, this would be an ethical conflict. I would have to wait to see how things played out. We were not scheduled for trial for three months. I explained all this to Carmen. She nodded. We probably had discovered more than we wanted to know.

The next troubling issue was what Avery might do at trial. He could always remain silent, in which case Ms. Jackson would bury him. If he took the stand, he might try self-defense, as well as a set up for the drugs in his car. It seemed that that was where he was heading. It was a huge risk and meant about 20 years or more in the slammer if he lost.

One of the most common techniques lawyers use is

obfuscation. When Ms. Jackson took the stand, she would not be able to explain how Avery ended up on the wrong side of the street and up the block. She would also not be convincing when she said she did not know where the drug house was. These issues, while irrelevant to the main case, when jumbled in her testimony would all sound strange. Was she protecting someone? Maybe the drug house, out of fear. All you need is reasonable doubt. For a handsome clean cut guy like Avery, maybe a jury could find it. I would have to befuddle Ms. Jackson on the stand.

Aliyah in the Office

It was a quiet day in the office. I shuffled through the phone messages, proofread my letters and two briefs. Angelina was pecking away just outside my door. Laura Lewis Iannelli, out office manager, said sotto voce, "Peter, we got one of yours our front. Are you busy?"

Most of our office handled corporate or estate matters, handled by compulsive guys with bland personalities. My work, not necessarily by choice, involved emotional disputes including divorces. It paid the bills. It entertained Angelina and it could wear me out. Fortunately, Angelina enjoyed the intrigue and took up much of the unproductive hand holding these clients required.   It was an office joke that any female sitting in our lobby and crying copious tears had to be my client.

"Who is she? Send her back."

"Aliyah Rosen." I wished then I had said I was very busy. When Angelina heard the name, she blurted out a "woo-hoo." She was about to hear some drama and especially on me. This had to be good.

Angelina jumped to her feet, nearly knocking over Laura in her rush to escort Aliyah back.

Aliyah was standing in the doorway with dark glasses, heaving a few shudders. I motioned for Angelina to shut the door. Alison, now Aliyah, had put on a few pounds, not much, her breasts were bigger. She was wearing lime green yoga pants, a white tank top and a leather jacket. I motioned for her to sit down. Then over our office intercom, I could hear that Angelina had put on Tammy Wynette singing "Stand by Your

Man." Very funny! She usually had opera on very discretely. Now was a good time to be ironic.

"Angie." "What?

"You know what."

"Aw, okay. Do you want me to take notes?" "No. I'll be okay."

Aliyah sat. We had not seen each other in maybe 15 years since she broke our engagement after I went into the military. It had long since passed. I was happily married to Lynn, the mother of my two boys. She taught music in middle school and loved it.

I repeated this to myself as a vision of one of my sexual exploits with Alison forced its way into my head – an uninhibited romp on the green of a nearby golf course just after dark. We left several dents on the immaculate green carpet. As this faded, I heard Aliyah say, "Peter, I'm sorry to bother you." (Yeah, sure I thought.)

"What can I do for you?"

"The car. My father is mad at me for losing the car he got me. He wants it back."   As she spoke I could see an obvious black eye mark on her left cheek with heavy makeup. I couldn't stop myself from asking.

"Did he hit you?" She looked at her feet and fiddled with a letter opener on my desk. "Are you gloating? Are you happy to see me like this?"

"No, I'm really not." (Well, maybe I was.) How did this happen? Do you need a restraining order?"

"No. I left all his things in a box outside the apartment in the hallway." "When?"

"After that hearing thing I went to."

"So you don't think he has a chance." (I knew she wasn't the long suffering type.)

"No. Not only is he a goner, but he got my car confiscated or something."

"Impounded. When it's used in the commission of a crime, they can impound it and sell it."

"But it's my car. I didn't shoot anyone."

"Well, it's the drugs in the spare tire well."

"But I didn't know it was there. I didn't know he was even dealing. He hid his money from me until I found it after that raid on the apartment. I had to stand outside the door in my nightie."

Another flashback – inadvertent. A pink silk teddy, her standing at her bedroom door waving me in as her parents left to go to a movie. I was in a three piece suit direct from law school. Her dressed in a teddy, me fully clothed as we wrestled out of our coverings. Come back, Peter! I pulled myself back. Ah, the car, yes the car.

"We can't use Avery to testify for you. He'd have to say they were his drugs. He can't do that. We'd have to go on your story alone. When was the last time you were near the rear tire wheel well?"

"Never."

"Never?"

"Yeah. The car was new. Andy may have. He brought his DJ stuff in the trunk sometimes."

"Could you afford an Audi?"

"Well, it's just an A3, but no, my father bought it for me."
"Where do you work and what do you make?"

"I do illustrations at the advertizing department of Macy's. I make about $15 an hour.

So, happy now? Big deal lawyer!"

"Whoa, whoa easy. If your father bought it, it may help the case. What did Avery make?"

"Not much. Mostly cash under the table." "So you were basically paying the bills?"

"You are enjoying this aren't you, Peter?" I guess I was.   I started to look at her. Yes, she was wearing what must have been a fashionable leather jacket a few years ago, but now it had scuff marks on the cuffs and elbows. Her white tank top was tight, but was on the grayish side. Still a wonderful rack, but a bit lower. My mind drifted once again to the parking lot outside a law school dance with us groping one another at the very edge of the parking lot.

It was dawning on me, as it had over the years, that our relationship was mostly physical. Nothing wrong with that, but we also fought a good bit. She didn't like my law school friends until they got drunk. They were sometimes pompous. She wanted me to wear the high style designer fashions. Lawyers wore preppy. As someone said, if you want to be a good lawyer, "Dress British, think Yiddish." She enjoyed shocking them. It did give me some street cred at that time. I remember we had a discussion about the ERA and there were just a smattering of female law students then and some knowledgeable wives. Alison, bless her heart, thought we were talking about earned run average, not the equal rights amendment. I could talk baseball with her and went to the Phillies a few times. She tried to get the attention of the camera that shoots the crowd by some dirty dancing moves. She never got on the screen, but those near us were quite pleased.

So anyway, this Avery was her latest choice. He was living off her and stashing the money he made from dealing drugs.

"So, I'm guessing he hit you when he realized you found his stash and were going to keep it.

"You got that right."

"So that black eye may be good evidence. If you were to testify that you had a fight after the drugs were discovered and the car was impounded. Could we take a picture of your eyes?"

"Sure, but only for you and the court."

I buzzed Angelina. "Angie, bring your camera."

Not only Angelina, but also Carmen burst through the door. They had been waiting outside. Too good to pass up.

"Angelina, can you take a picture of her black eye without the eye makeup?" "I'll get the camera while she washes off the makeup."

Carmen had been eyeing Alison up and down. "I'll take her to the ladies room."

All three returned shortly. "Peter, he also hit me on the chest," she said, pulling up her tank top. She had on a skimpy bra which hooked in the front. I said a silent prayer for all bras that hooked in the front. My mind started to drift to another of our scenes, but I was able to pull it back only to see her two bare breasts with the left one having a large black and blue mark with knuckle prints. Before I could say anything, Angelina was snapping away and turning Alison this way and that. Alison enjoyed the attention and the provocative posing.

"Any other bruises?" Angelina asked.

"No, just the eye." Her left eye had some blood on the pupil. Angelina got that.

Carmen gave me the nod of approval for Aliyah's ample breasts with a sign uplifting her own and winking.

"Uh, that's enough ladies." I said motioning to the door for Angelina and Carmen, who reluctantly slunk out, sorry to miss all the fun. Alison/Aliyah stood and started to cry again, but did not put her top back on. Fortunately, I was too smart for this. I stayed behind my desk.

"Oh, Peter, I have screwed up things," she said as she picked up her tank top. She knew Andy was going to prison and would be looking to replace him. Somebody with a few bucks. Whoever in the world could that be?

"I don't like this Avery character. He's looking at substantial jail time."

"I don't have anybody in my life now. Could we have dinner sometime?"

I had now smacked my face mentally a few times. I knew the answer to this question. "Look, I'll file a motion to get your car back. We have a decent chance of winning."

"So, will I owe you anything?" Fortunately, I knew the answer to this one too.

"No, I'll do what I can. Tell your father I said hello." Her father was a nice fellow. He was devastated when we broke up.

She was now putting her eye makeup back on and reaching forward for her pocketbook.

I was learning. I didn't lean forward to look as her unhooked breasts dangled.

As she walked out the door, now fully reassembled, she

thanked Angelina.

When she was well down the hallway, Angelina came in and pulled the door shut. She started, "You . . ."

"Angie, I got it. She's off limits. I got it." Angelina came from a very religious Italian family and she had divorced her husband for having an affair. She ignored his many pleas to come back. I knew where she stood. But I knew where I stood. This was going nowhere.

Carmen stuck her head in the door. "Is she gone?"

"Yes," snapped Angelina. "Yes, she is. And don't ask stupid questions." Carmen retreated and all was quiet.

I still shuddered at a particular incident at Bobby Friedman's Bar Mitzvah. Alison and I had both been invited as we were considered a couple by the Friedmans. Her dad was Bobby's orthodontist whose work would be on gleaming display from the pulpit. The Friedmans vaguely knew my parents. So to Blooming Twig Country Club we both went in late March. I had, of course, worn a conservative suit and she had a long peach silk kind of suit jacket. She did look splendid in it, but a bit garish. With the service over, we were herded to a large side room where drinks and hors d'oeuvres were on offer. Alison belted back two white wines and I sipped a bloody Mary and chatted with some of the guests we knew. She held my arm proprietarily and unbuttoned the peach silk jack to reveal, and I mean reveal, a nicely tanned cleavage which drew the attention of most of the men and, not less than some of the women, as all the while she grinned by my side.

Soon the doors opened to the main ballroom and we were directed to our tables by place cards appropriately numbered. I was pleased to see we were not seated with the family discards, but the younger folks. Dr. and Mrs. Rosen stopped by on their way to the second main table as honored guests of the Friedmans. Since I was descended from Russian Jews, I did not have the exalted standing in this assembly of German Jews, now at least three generations or more in America, while I was maybe late second generation. Alison's mother gasped at this peach silk number on my date and spat out, "Alison, what were you thinking?" Alison shrugged. In the scheme of things, Alison's capture of me, an Ivy League graduate and law school student was her redemption, so I smiled manfully an apology to her mother, and her father clapped me on the back on the way to the prestigious second main table.

While a salad of spring mix and apricot vinaigrette dressing was being disbursed, the band struck up. Alison grabbed my arm and we were among the first on the dance floor. I could feel all eyes on us as Alison jiggled in her décolletage and exhibited a few moves which belied a complete lack of bone structure between her knees and her navel. On the subsequent slow number, she had us entwined in a manner reminiscent of several pages of the Kama Sutra of Vatsayama. We could well adorn any of many temples in India. Since we were in a German Jewish conservative Bar Mitzvah celebration, we not, I felt, not quite so honored. As the beat of the music picked up, the dancers separated and did their "own thing." Alison's consisted in part of twerking the congregation president as I danced opposite his wife, a prominent fixture in Hadassah. The band subsided, we returned the spring mix salads. After some much appreciated quiet time for conversation, the band struck up again as the wait staff served the salmon or London broil at the place settings. Our table of younger adults again all rose to dance, but the friends of the bar mitzvah boy by now had taken over the dance floor and some hired entertainment were organizing contests for the teeny boppers. It was not the time to watch the kids, because conversation was once again impossible over the din. Without an opportunity to show herself in her peach ensemble, Alison was ready to leave, as was I. As we waited for our valet parking assistant to bring us my car, I had a range of mixed feelings. I was, yes, embarrassed by the, shall I say, extroversion, of Alison. Something male in me wanted my woman to be reserved and original, but something told me she was hot. I was, I guess, in lust, in love, infatuation, but certainly beyond rational thought. Alison was in more than her usual state of arousal and the peach thingy was cast aside at her dorm room at the art school she attended.

I did notice a peculiar reaction to my recent social display. I had advanced from sturdy husband material with my academic achievements and conservative suit all the way to bad boy. And women can rarely resist a bad boy. I had acquired a street cred, a rep as a sexual being, and a forbidden fruit. Well, not fruit exactly. Over the next several weeks, I was getting glances from some of the females at the "young adults" table and, a few brushes with breasts on my back and shoulders. That summer, we were invited to a new social life, mostly arranged by the young women.

Back in the Office – Avery with News

Following Alison's visit, things in the office quieted down except for a few You Tube articles appearing on my computer about Delilah, Lilith and Jezebel (a few more versions of Stand by Your Man), courtesy of Angelina.. Angelina had been hard at work. The routine matters in the office for moneyed corporate clients paid lots of bills. I did the litigation for a variety of corporate or commercial disputes – defective products, theft of corporate secrets, partnership breakups, - lots of money, not much drama. People who think litigation is exciting do not understand that most cases settle after mounds and mounds of paperwork and billable hours are generated.

So when Avery came in unannounced with a midday news report on his phone, it caused some stir. He was back to the black t-shirt, obscure heavy metal rock band tour imprint and an unkempt dissipated look. While I was not happy about having to do a favor for Alison to get her car, I could not condone Avery's domestic violence – the act of a coward; one more piece of derogatory evidence of his character. I can't say I was upset to see a few scratch marks on his forehead.

"So, how did the fight with Aliyah turn out, Andy?" He had come in to the office full of some good news apparently and had been punctured by my question.

"Not so good. I got thrown out and she stole my money. Can I sue for that?"

"You mean the money you got from drug sales you never told her about while she supported you?"

"Yes, well. But that was my money." "On which you paid taxes?"

"Well, no."

"So you want the court to have her turn over this untaxed money so the drug enforcement people can claim it as the proceeds of a continuing drug operation?"

"Oh, I see. Ok, well, never mind. But look at this on my phone. Ms. Jackson was shot! She can't testify."

I looked at the blurb of news from a local station. Sure enough, Ms. Jackson was lying in the street outside a school building with some police standing around. They had a blanket over her and there were some school kids in the background being interviewed by a reporter. It appeared that she was dead. I looked up at Avery.

"Why is this good?"

"She can't testify against me. Don't you see? My boys took care of me."

A major forehead slap. "No, you idiot. She already has testified and been under cross- examination by your lawyer. I can't cross examine her now at trial."

"You mean that hearing thing? They can use that?"

"Yes. They just read the transcript into the record"

"They can do that?"

"Yes. It seems your boys haven't protected you." "Hmm, not good."

"Yes, I was planning a full cross for her at trial to bring out the confusion as to where your body was found, on the wrong side of the street, away from the drug house. Now, I can't do that."

"Oh."

"Yeah, oh. Now would be a good time for you to start cooperating with me instead of your drug gang idiots. I mean you are looking at major time if you are convicted. I can't help you if you don't tell me what is going on." He stared off into space turning his head side to side.

"Are we confidential?"

"Yes, of course. But look, don't waste my time. I don't want to find you've made something up."

"Okay, okay. I've been a DJ for a couple years now. The pay is lame. Really lame and just a few nights a week."

"Can you do something else?"

"Not really. I dropped out of college. I can do construction." "You mean as a laborer, not skilled."

"Yeah."

"Could you get skilled?"

"My father paid for some plumbing apprentice stuff, but I didn't like it." "Okay, so you DJ. And I guess you sell drugs?"

"Yeah. The Penn and Drexel kids know me and the high school kids at the raves. I carry everything – weed, coke, PCP, meth and other pills."

"So you get supplied by this house on Apple." "Yeah."

"So why go to shoot them up?"

"Okay, so this black/Spanish dude starts talking at the rave gig saying my bag is short. He's got a little scale and he starts weighing them. I mean out in public. So we start to argue. Then he wants me to join his gang and buy from him. He'll give me $120 out of a batch of ten instead of 100. I think I'm being set up so I say no, but I'm gonna ask my guys on Apple. So I decide not to ask them, but I'll tell them their bags are short like the guy said. So I talk to Pug Dog at the house and he gets mad. He starts waving a bat. So, I don't take a bat to a gun fight, I get out my gun. We are shouting and the guy on the second floor is shushing us both.   He doesn't want the whole block to hear. I may have said something about this dude at the rave weighing a bag I sold him. Then, I'm shot in the shoulder. I fall to my side and start shooting at Pug Dog. I fall again and somebody hits me with the bat. That's all I remember until the hospital.

"Did you say anything to the police?"

"No. I know better than that."

"Can you ID the guy from the rave that weighed your bag?"

"Sure. That's Flacco. A half Spanish guy."

"Was he selling at the rave too?"

"He was trying to, but I had my own crowd. College kids, they knew me not to sell them shit."

"So, have you been talking to Pug Dog's gang?"

"Yeah. They say to play it cool. They'll get me off. I guess they think without that lady up the block they can't make a case."

"Like I said, they were wrong."

"Thanks. A little late."

"But they have always been saying 'don't snitch.' If they can kill her, I guess they can kill me."

"Ah, now the dawn breaks. Yes. You are small potatoes."

"So I should lay low."

"Absolutely."

"But then they'll think I'm gonna snitch."

"Get a burn phone and tell them you are lying low and won't snitch."

"I could do that. But do I snitch?"

"I'm guessing that's your best bet, but not so fast. Let me see some more about this case.

I'll go talk to the DA and see what's up."

"So what about Aliyah?"

"What about her?"

"They will check out her apartment."

"Not after you gave her a black eye."

"It's not the first time. We've gotten back together before."

"Andy, you are a classy dude."

"Yeah well. She says she was once tight with you, but dumped you way back when."

"True enough."

"Well, she's never dumped me."

"Yeah. Go figure."

"Without me around, she may want you back."

"No way!"

"She can be persuasive."

"Andy, no way that will happen." I couldn't tell whether he was tempting me now, or was trying to tell me to keep my hands off.

"Look, Andy, I'll get her car back and then that's it."

"I feel bad she lost the car. Can I help? You know, as a gesture that I'm sorry." I had to think about that for a while. Maybe if his mother came and said he had been living with her since prior to the shooting, it might show she hadn't had the car. I told him I was going to show they had a fight and she had a black eye.

"She had it coming."

"How's that?"

"She took my money." I wasn't going to argue that point. I just shrugged and shook my head.

He eventually left and said he'd call me on a burn phone. I kept wondering why I would represent a scum bag like this. First, I guess because I was a sworn lawyer and had a duty to protect a client. And really, two, I didn't like to lose. But I could feel greater revulsion for him and for myself the more he spoke. If I had to voice a personal opinion, I would see him in jail for 20 years in the hard time wing; but our system wasn't supposed to work that way. I had to be a good scout.

Car Hearing

Angelina had already sent out the hearing notice for the Motion for Return of Property to consider the status of Alison's Audi A3. It was for mid-June. We were able to get Avery's mother to show up to testify as to Avery's residence at the time of the shooting and the estrangement of her son from Alison. A few days before, we were notified that the hearing would be at the afternoon session in Courtroom 653.

So Alison, now Aliyah, showed up at the hearing on time. She was dressed in a long peasant skirt, Birkenstocks and a pink blouse with an embroidered jean jacket. Her hair was not straight as it was back in the 70's. As she came up to me, I could notice a discernible sway to her breasts; she was now retro braless. Why the homage to that era I don't know, or pretended not to. She insisted on giving me a warm peck on the cheek as we sat in the back row of the courtroom and rubbed her breasts on my arm. As they called the list for the calendar, we were one of the last, so it could be a long day.

The judge was to be Henry O'Rourke, a pleasant young fellow with ties to politicians. Never a great lawyer, he was given these minor assignments over the years as lawyers discovered his mediocrity. He had acquired "black robe disease" in which he now could lord it over lawyers who came into his court and belittle them. Since the hearing was in front of a judge alone, he alone could make the decision on the facts. Their only recourse would be to ask for a full blown jury trial. Since the amounts at issue in these cases were small, his decision alone reigned supreme. Of course, Judge O'Rourke showed up late and kept a full courtroom waiting.

The good news, however, was that a change had taken place on the issue of impoundment. In the past, the prosecutor and the police split the proceeds from the sale of confiscated objects, but a newspaper article exposed that there was some corruption in the handling of these funds. There was also pressure on the judges to enrich the pockets of those two entities, the District Attorney and the police who appeared in court on a regular basis. After the article, the courts were much more lenient in returning the property to its original owners. I hoped that such would be the case today. Really mediocre judges rarely rocked the boat and followed the now regular practice.

About 3:30, I got a bleep on my phone from Angelina. I took it outside.

"Peter, it seems you're going to dinner and a show at the Arden tonight with Lynn."

"That's right."

"Lynn called. She's done early and is taking the train in after her last class."

"Ok."

"I told her to go to Courtroom 653 in City Hall where you are with . . . with . . , I forget."

"Angie!"

"What?"

"You know."

"Oh yes, you are with Jezebel."

"No. Aliyah Rosen."

"Oh, that's right. So Aliyah in Room 653."

I don't know whether Angelina thought she was protecting

me from myself or just enjoyed creating drama. She probably thought both.

Our case was finally called about 4:00 p.m. so Aliyah and I went to the counsel table and sat. Ms. Witherspoon sat in the front room waiting to be called as a witness.

Judge O'Rourke nodded to me. "Proceed, counsel."

"Your Honor, we seek the return of my client's car that was impounded by the police in March. An Avery Witherspoon was arrested on a charge of drugs and other offenses and the car he was driving impounded as being the instrument of a crime. Ms. Rosen was not in the car at the time, and did not participate in any drug transaction, nor did she know that there were any drugs in the car. In fact, she and Avery Witherspoon have been estranged for some time; he was then living with his mother in Villanova."

The court turned to the Assistant District Attorney, "Counsel, your response." The ADA then went into all the gruesome details alleged by the police, reciting from the police 49's the shooting, and the search of the car. He hoped to show what a vicious criminal Avery was and cast doubt on Aliyah's claim of innocence.

It had been a long day for O'Rourke, so he wearily turned back to me and said, "Your witness, counselor."

I had prepared Alison/Aliyah carefully by going over the questions I would ask her and how best she should answer them. I felt confident she would be a good witness for herself, so I started with the first question. "Do you know Avery Witherspoon?" With that, she released a torrent of information, some helpful, some not.

"We had been living together for a few years, but I threw

him out on March 16. He was DJing at some raves on Lancaster Avenue near Penn and hitting on the young girls. I was paying the rent and the groceries and he sometimes paid out of his DJ money. I never knew he got money from selling drugs. So anyway, he went to live with his mother and borrowed my car until, as he said, he could get on his feet. I can take the el to my job, so I didn't need it during the week, but he kept it on the weekend too.

"When he got arrested we had a major blow up and he hit me several times. I have pictures." She turned to me for the envelope with the pictures and handed them up to the judge. The judge looked at the batch, including the black eye and the breast with the knuckle marks. He lingered over the picture of the breast.

"So, Ms. Rosen, where do you work?"

"At the ad agency Tuohy and Taubman, Eighth and Chestnut."

He looked closely at her and seemed to realize she was braless now as she squirmed nervously or maybe jiggled intentionally. He put the photos down on the space before him.

"So," he looked at me.

"So, Your Honor, she was not involved in the drug transaction, now or any time in the past, and did not know of the drugs in the car."

"Cross, counsel"

The young ADA got up. "So these drugs were not yours?"

"In no way."

"But you had been living with him for several years and you did not know he was dealing?"

"No. Most of the fight had been about how I was supporting

him while he had all this drug money."

"Why didn't you file charges after he hit you?" "I wanted to be rid of him once and for all." "No further questions."

The judge turned to me. "Any further witnesses counselor?"

"I offer Mrs. Witherspoon, Avery Witherspoon's mother who will say that at the time of the incident, he was living with her."

"Fine, we'll accept your representation. Clerk, make out an order returning the automobile to Ms. Aliyah Rosen. Do we have her address?"

"Yes, judge."

"Fine, next case."

It was that simple. The law had changed over the years, the property of probably innocent people, parents, wives, girlfriends, etc. was no longer confiscated unless an actual connection to the crime could be shown. But I got a big hug from Aliyah as we turned to go with a certificate of the order returning the car.

As we walked down the aisle, my wife Lynn stood and greeted us.

"Honey, this is Aliyah Rosen. My wife Lynn." There was a pause as they inspected each other like lionesses. Lynn was dressed in her usual outfit, black jeans, a white turtleneck and a sweater. Aliyah now appearing as the retro hippy and braless.

"Nice guy you have here," said Aliyah.

"So I've found," said Lynn. Lynn was mild mannered and soft spoken, but was able to make herself known. I knew I was not going to hear the end of this. Alison, now Aliyah, with the retro hippy look and the braless look in the well air conditioned courtroom. It was a wealth of wisecracks for the years.

Fortunately, I had already told Lynn about this incarnation of Aliyah. I could just shake my head as I stood to weather the remarks. I pondered the mysteries of life: how demons are implanted in our psyches which can lead us to destruction; how events outside our control can save us or doom us; how mysterious is human existence. My thoughts returned to reality as I followed Lynn to the el and our restaurant before the Arden production. Alison/Aliyah waved her certificate at me as she went to get an Uber to the impound lot.

Lunchtime Warning

In the quiet period between crises, I was able to plow through mounds of paperwork we lawyers inflict on each other in civil cases. Somehow, we believe that we can force opposing counsel to ignore a deadline, or suffer some life altering event which will help our client win a case not based on the facts or justice. So we lob from our word processing trebuchete an unending barrage of motions, or discovery requests, expert witness interrogatories, or manufactured crises to keep each other awake in the middle of the night as we recount the myriad of details we must attend to the next day or have forgotten from the previous day. The heap on my desk and credenza began to diminish. I pushed back from the desk and went to my safe haven, the gym. I could pump iron and hang out with some of my gym buddies. And then to lunch at one of my favorite stops where the waitress knew my name and my order – tuna, white toast, Dr. Brown black cherry. I was now calm and in a euphoric endorphin-induced state. I read a Daily News someone had left behind and mused over the opinion some sports writer had issued to cause shock and dismay among Philly sports fans. The truth never mattered to him – only an apoplectic response from his readers.

Then, a roughly dressed, thin Hispanic guy came up and sat in my booth facing me and flicked a page of the paper. I looked up to see a man in his 30's with a Dallas Cowboys baseball hat on backwards and some major bling hanging from his neck to the wife-beater tank at his chest.

"Yo, Stern." He had my attention, as well as that of my waitress who looked at me with alarm.

"What do you want, Mr.?

"Yo, Stern . . . you working for Avery Witherspoon?" I was now on high alert, but called on all my thug movie cool.

"What's it to you?"

"Yo." (Somehow Rocky Balboa's favorite word had leaked into every Philly sentence and crossed cultural lines.) "We paid for you, so we got some say."

"How's that?" I was not going into a review of the Canon of Ethics as to what fiduciary duties I owed to whom. In street parlance, he felt he had hired me. It was always better to hear him out than fight.

"So, the 5k we gave his mom was ours. It was for a trial, not a plea."

"Ah-ha! A trial costs a lot more. That 5K got you through a preliminary hearing and an investigation of the facts. A jury trial goes for more. At least $35k for maybe a week's trial."

"Yeah. We got that. We want a trial, no plea you hear."

"Ok, I can always do a trial, but he could lose and do major time."

"A trial, that's what we want. No plea, no cooperation." He exaggerated this last word as if each syllable left a bitter taste in his mouth. Now, we were getting to the crux of the matter. If Avery cooperated, he would try to rat out the entire organization he worked for, and hope for a favorable deal from the DA and the judge. I knew his case was a bad one, but good information could get him out in three to five years of soft time, while a losing trial effort would cost him the rest of his life at some decrepit upstate max prison with some very bad dudes looking at his comely white ass. It was clearly my advice that he should cooperate and reduce his time in prison. He had given me nothing to go on, and didn't even want to talk to me in the beginning. It was obvious that his advisers were his drug gang. I was curious as to why they wanted to back him now. Of course, he must have some dirt on them, but after all, he had shot up Pug Dog and involved one of their drug houses in some notoriety even if his body had been dragged from the site. But the drug house was protected, it seems, by regular payments to the narco cops, and the site itself could easily be moved to another location. It must be that Avery was a good producer for them and gave them good access to the college kids' raves on Lancaster Avenue. A black street guy was easily replaced. A white guy who had access to the college market was unique, even with a shootout. But with a trial, he could go away for a long time. Why did they need him then? Had some deal been made? These drug guys were not the brightest. They killed off Ms. Jackson for a dumb reason, her testimony was preserved and I lost the opportunity to screw her up on cross. The most obvious reason for them to help Avery was to prevent him from ratting out their organization.

"Okay, a trial you get. But it costs."

"Yeah. We know. You'll get your money." He slipped out of the booth and was gone. Joe, the restaurant owner and chief sandwich maker, came over, "Are you alright Mr. Stern?"

"Yeah, yeah, I'm fine. Joe, have you got any cameras here? I wonder if I could get a shot of him."

"Mr. Stein, I got cameras out the wazoo."

"Could I burn a few CD's from today's lunch time."

"No sweat. I'll get the tech guy. He's my cousin. He set me up good."

I went back to the office. All endorphins gone. I placed a call to Henry Thompson, a chief inspector in the Police Department. He was a buddy of mine from the gym. I could get him to ID this guy from the drug gang.

"So, Pete, what's up?"

"I represent Avery Witherspoon in a matter involving a

shooting on Apple Street at a drug house there. Someone is paying his fee and is threatening me, Henry, This guy came to talk to me where I usually eat lunch. I can get a CD of him and wondered if you could ID him."

"Sure, no sweat, Pete. Some outside evidence could help if you want to cooperate.

"Bingo, Henry, Just my thought. And witness intimidation into the bargain."

"You got it, Peter. Send over the CD when you can."

I went back to the office with lots on my mind. Who was this guy? Would Thompson have anything on him. I was sure there was an intelligence file on him somewhere. As I walked past the reception area, Laura Lewis Iannello was standing by her office door with a curious smile on her face. She was a classy lady whose major expertise was handling estate matters for wealthy older clients, the lifeblood of our firm. Her hair was immaculately coiffed in a frosted blond, her gold earrings shimmered and set off her silk maize and rust suit. It was rumored that she was quite wealthy but just enjoyed her job. She was holding a neatly wrapped wad of hundreds.

"Peter Stern, you are a piece of work." She knew my area of legal expertise differed from the other lawyers and bordered on the edge of social norms, to put it politely, as she always did.

"What did I do now?" I had reverted to my naughty school boy persona when confronted with this proper and fashionable image our office wished to project.

She waved me into her office where a large plastic Easter bunny had been opened and stacks of wrapped $100 bills spilled across. A note attached said "Thirty pieces of silver."

"Actually, it was $35,000, but close enough. What's this for?"

"My fee for representing Avery Witherspoon in a jury trial. Paid up front."

"So what do I do? Put it in escrow until after the trial?"

"Actually, I would wash it. It may have some residue of coke on it. I'd hate to see you attacked by a German shepherd with a trained nose."

"My God, Peter, what are you into?"

"Sorry, Laura. It's the way criminal fees come in. Up front and in cash. Did you give the guy a receipt?"

"No, he handed it to Eloise at the front desk and left."

"Can we get a CD of him as he comes in?"

"Sure, I guess so."

"Who was he?"

"A messenger from the Dogs Out Gang. You know 'Who Let the Dogs Out'. Woof Woof!"

"Peter, are we in danger."

"No, Laura, unless you sniff your fingers and get too high to do estate tax returns."

"Wha!" she recoiled.

"Just kidding. I'm sure they knew to wash the bills. Otherwise they can be traced."

"I swear, Peter . . ."

"Put the cash in the vault until I earn it. Don't touch the bills if you can avoid it. They may have fingerprints."

"Gack!" She dropped the stack she was holding and got out a plastic bag and a pair of rubber kitchen gloves from her desk,

"You haven't gotten us into something terrible have you?"

"No, it's the way criminal law is practiced."

"Can't you bring us in a nice dim old dowager with a mammoth estate?"

"Maybe in 20 years. How about a weepy divorce client, male or female?"

"Ok, I'll take them."

"Thanks Laura. I'm going in to see Digby. I have a few issues on this matter.”

“Thank God, a voice of reason.”

I stopped by Angelina’s desk. “Anything up?”

“Not much.”

“I’m going to see Digby about Avery.”

I walked up to the corner office guarded by Ms. James, Digby’s personal assistant and guard dog. “Betty, can I see Digby for a second?”

“He’s on a short call. He’ll be off soon.”

When the light went off on her desk, she waved me in.

“So, Peter, how is everything?”

“Fine. Just have a small complication I want to run by you.” “Sit. Let’s hear it.”

Digby Bradenton was the firm’s senior partner, a double Harvard man, undergrad and law, and known and respected around Philadelphia. He had practiced all levels of law on the way up to what was the quiet pasture of estates and trusts. He knew every prominent republican in town, was on a weekly lunch basis with the Episcopal Church Archbishop and knew all the big deal CEO’s in town on a first name basis. For me, he was both a father confessor and chief rabbi.

So I laid out the facts of Avery Witherspoon’s representation, shooting, arrest, refusal to cooperate, Aliyah/Alison, and now my lunchtime confrontation.

“So, I have received a $35,000 retainer for a jury trial for Avery from the Dogs Out Gang, whose messenger told me no ‘cooperation,’ just a trial.” I imitated the facial grimace attending the attenuated pronunciation of cooperation.

“I get your problem. You represent Avery. He is the client. The drug gang is now overt in paying our fee and has demanded a trial and not a guilty plea with cooperation to get a reduced sentence.”

As usual, Digby grasped the facts and the issues quickly and neatly.

"So, what do you do? It is absolutely clear that you represent Avery and Avery alone, not the Dog Gang. So you must give him your best advice, which I get from the recital of facts is that he should plead guilty and cooperate."

"I agree and have told him so before we got our retainer."

"So ethically, we are in the clear. Avery can do what he wants. But what does this connection with the Dog Gang mean? Do we owe them anything?"

"Exactly my question."

"Noting trumps your duty to you client." He mused staring at the ceiling. His back was to an expansive view of North Philadelphia and the Delaware River. I almost could hear wheels turning as he ground through a number of thoughts. "Of course, if he goes to trial it doesn't matter. You have complied with their contingency. Now, do you have a contract with them? In a sense you do, but it is against public policy for them to compel you to breach your duty of trust with your client; so it is not a contract which can be enforced. Now, if you take their money, and then he pleads guilty, should you return the money? First, they are asking you to commit a criminal act – obstruction of justice. Did you ever agree to accept the money on the affirmative understanding that you would not cooperate?"

"No. He told me what he wanted and then delivered the money in cash to the office." "So you made no affirmative representations?"

"No. He said what he had to say and left."

"Interesting. Peter, do some research. Find out if someone receives a bribe and then defaults on the corrupt promise. Let's first think this through." I could hear the wheels turning as he returned again to whatever thoughts the ceiling above might give him. As a practical matter, if you do cooperate and keep the money, you are in a shitload of trouble with a lot of bad guys. So, we don't need to research the law of the jungle. We already know that."

"Simple answer. Don't make a move now. Let's wait and see what happens. Personally, I don't want to have you hurt over $35,000 to our firm. So go and sin no more."

"Got it, Digby. I'll keep you posted."

I walked back to my office reconsidering our options.

Conference with D.A.

The next step in the process was a conference with the DA's office to schedule a trial or discuss a possible guilty plea. I had no feedback as yet from Avery, so I would see what options we had and then call him in to talk.

My conference was at 10:30 at the DA's office next to the courthouse. As I walked in, my heart sank. My Assistant DA for the trial was Martha Liederkranz. A nerdy lady with dull straight mousy hair and a J.C. Penney's Hilary pantsuit in light gray. She actually wore matching gray Hush Puppies. She was a person devoid of all imagination and dedicated to exacting every ounce of justice for the Commonwealth of Pennsylvania. She lacked the ability to negotiate anything. I guessed she simply had no confidence and wanted to have the jury and the court make all decisions. Even at trial, her extreme positions on interpreting the facts cost her points with most juries. Yet she had been in the DA's office for years and no one could question her honesty or her work ethic. However, in large cities, the courts cannot afford the luxury of trying every case to a jury. It would tie up the court calendar so that effective justice would never get done, and the cost of tying up the judge, his staff, the cost would be overwhelming. Over 90% of most cases resulted in guilty pleas and ended all appeals. So, Ms. Liederkranz was a luxury the system could ill afford. Therefore, my barely audible groan as she brought her case file in.

She was pleasant enough. She went down the list of all the witnesses she would present, all the documentary and physical exhibits, with a concealed smugness. She knew she had a winning case and wanted a stat for the time promotions or raises were discussed.

"Mr. Stern . . ."

"Please, call me Pete."

"Ok, Peter. I think we have a solid case here. We read in Ms. Jackson's testimony from the Preliminary Hearing, the shell casing analysis, the gun powder residue test, the drug analysis of the drugs in the Audi A3, obtained with a search warrant." She was rummaging through her file, pulling out copies of the documents already marked by exhibit numbers.

"Ms. Liederkranz," I paused waiting for her to tell me her name was Martha. It was not forthcoming, so I continued. "Look, he's a handsome white kid who got caught in a bad neighborhood with the Who Let the Dogs Out gang, buying a minor stash and got mugged."

"Nice try, counsel. We know he was a DJ at a rave on Lancaster Avenue and was selling addictive drugs to college kids and underage minors."

"Where'd you get that?"

"The cops know about the raves."

"How can you get that in?"

"At sentencing. He also beats up his girl friend and she lets him have her car for his drug business." Unfortunately, the evidence presented at sentencing is not "beyond a reasonable doubt" and comes from anywhere without real proof. Just say the word "Confidential informant" and the judge can hear it.

"So, Peter." I had the feeling I was being reprimanded by my third grade teacher. "We got Avery on aggravated assault, a variety of drugs and weapons violations. I figure he will die an old man in a bad prison."

At that point, Lou Dawson, head of the major trials unit, walked in. "May I join you two?" Lou was in his early 30s, well dressed and a political protégé of the elected DA who was looking to go on to other things. Lou was a decent fellow and could be trusted to make a deal. He saw 'deal' written all over this case and knew Ms. Liedenkranz would be a stumbling block.

"Of course, Lou. How have you been?"

"Good Pete. You don't come to the criminal side enough. So I've reviewed the case summary, Pete. Doesn't look good." He looked at Martha and nodded.

"So, Lou . . . Martha . . . what can we do here?"

"Can you proffer anything good on the Dog Gang, Pete? We can always use some inside information."

"Certainly, he knows all the guys in the house on Apple."

"Our narco cops already have that and, unfortunately, the shooting scattered them to other locations. So it would be nice, but not very helpful. What we would like would be a really nice lead into the drugs on the Penn and Drexel campuses. If we could get a video on some sales at the raves with Mr. Witherspoon wearing a wire. What do you think?

"I don't know. I'll ask. Can we postpone the trial listing for a while?" I thought Ms. Liederkranz might have a stroke, but Lou said 'sure'. He knew this case with very few witnesses was one he could put on as a backup filler, always handy when another case ended early, so he could keep this one on the back burner.

Conference with Avery Post Proffer and Plea Deal

I wasn't enthusiastic about our prospects for a plea deal, so I thought it best to bring in Avery for a frank discussion of his future.   Things looked bleak, he hadn't been cooperative in the past and I saw no reason to sugarcoat anything. Although I asked him to come in at 10:00 a.m., Avery wandered in at about 11:00. He had his usual black tee shirt from some forgotten heavy metal group and hadn't showered for several days.

"So, Avery . . ."

"Andy . . ."

"Sorry Andy, I think it's a good time to lay everything out on the table.   Things did not go well with my conference with the DA; they simply felt you had nothing of value to give them as part of a plea deal. We could always make what we call an open plea without a deal, and hope the judge gives you some points for that, but not much. So what's going on with you now."

"A couple of things. I got my old DJ job back and I moved back in with Aliyah."

"What? She let you back in?"

"What can I say? She isn't happy living by herself and I am a persuasive guy."

"Did she give you your drug money back?"

"Some. Some she kept for past and some for the future."

"Now, the DJ job, are you still selling drugs?"

"I got some left from my old stash. I got to keep my customers happy."

"Is that guy still at the rave, your competitor, that was

weighing your bags and telling you they were short weight?

"Yes, he's there; but the college kids like me better."

"You know if they catch you dealing, they'll revoke your bail and it would mean a lot more time on your sentence."

"I gotta do what I gotta do."

"Yeah, I get that."

"So, I got a few ideas. Who is this guy, your competitor, getting his supply from?"

"The west Philly guys. I think they are the Zombies or the Phantoms, something like that."

"Do you know any of them?"

"Maybe. They send someone around to get me to deal their stuff once in a while."

"Have you ever done it?"

"Nah. To much risk if the Dogs found out.

"But let's say you talk to them now."

"What do you mean?"

"Well, you're running out of your stash, aren't you?"

"Yeah, I'm low."

"So, maybe you buy from them."

"OK, then what"

"Then, they give us dirt on the Dogs. I'm sure they got some. You don't have anything on the Dogs now that the DA wants, do you?"

"No, I just know the guys in the house on Apple Street."

"And you shot one of them. I don't think they like you anymore."

"Well, not exactly. One of the bosses came by and he wants to keep me supplied."

"Even after all that?"

"What can I say. Business is business. I got a good route."

"I got another idea. How do you feel about cooperating with the cops and having your sales to the college kids video taped?"

"Why would I do that?"

"First, it gets you a very good deal. Second, we notify the parents of the kids. The cops would love that. Protect the kids. Their parents are paying $50,000 to send them to a good college and the kids are spending their allowances on gateway drugs."

"Sounds risky."

"True."

"But what do I do after that. I've killed off my clientele."

"Go straight. Get a normal job."

"I don't know about that."

"Otherwise, you're doing maybe 20 years hard time as somebody's girl friend."

"Yeah, yeah."

"You probably would have to leave town."

"Yeah, I'd have to think about this."

"Sure, we have time. But, look, I'm going to have an assistant of mine go to the rave and take pictures. I want you to point out your competitor there. I'll be there too in disguise. Don't give us away."

"No, I get that."

"So, go and think about it."

"Yeah, good."

"And don't hit Aliyah anymore."

"Still got a thing for her?"

"No. I don't think you should hit women."

"Heh, heh, sure."

"No, I mean it."

"Ok, ok.

This little plan was the one way I could think of to scare up some dirt on the Dogs and maybe get Avery a reduced sentence. I had no particular desire to help him as a human being. He was a scum bag, but I was bound as a lawyer to do the best I could. Somehow, I felt he probably deserved 20 years in jail, but that was not my job. He left. I buzzed Carmen and explained her job.

"So I mingle with all these rich preppy kids and take their photos buying drugs."

"Yeah, that part."

"And get this other guy selling drugs. Do I buy some myself?"

"No, you're not a cop. I don't want you charged with possession."

"Ok, piece of cake. Warm up my phone and get some party pics."

Rave Visit

The building where the rave was held was a large multi-story factory building. Its first floor was an immense floor with a 25 foot high ceiling. Along one end was a bar with four active bartenders and some high stools, at the other was a large seating area littered with old sofas, hassocks and chairs collected from the area's thrift stores. In the middle was a DJ stand about six feet above the main floor with wires of every sort stretching up to the ceiling and connected to speakers hanging on all four walls at random locations. The place was dimly lit in an assortment of different colored bulbs strung on wires from wall to wall. There were a few EXIT signs here and there, but there was a nightmare of safety and electrical violations throughout.

The upper floors were small gerry-rigged compartments which served as bedrooms for the permanent occupants. A few of the rooms had electrical feeds, some did not. As a new occupant would show up for the communal housing, he would nail a few pieces of plywood into some sort of enclosure and cordon off a bedroom for himself. Sometimes he would cobble together an illegal electric line off the box. Some built shelves, or cantilevered beds, some just slept on an old mattress. The permanent occupants had a variety of jobs, usually construction, or bartending – the under-the-table gig economy – untaxed, unregulated, unknown. They, however, divided the proceeds of the rave admissions and the bar. The DJ was paid some, but it was understood he made most of his money on the dope franchise. The kids loved it. Total freedom, anti-establishment and a throwback to the hippy era.

Rave with Carmen

I told Carmen she would be undercover at the rave and taking photos. She was born ready.

"So, Pete, this must include dinner at the Vecchio on Chestnut Street." Carmen was always up for a meal on the firm and I assured her she could indulge. Any after hours work at the firm usually included a meal.

"Do you need clothes to look like a Penn College kid?" After some thought, Carmen decided she already had the right wardrobe and didn't want to burden the firm's account any further.

Raves started late, maybe 11:00 p.m. at the earliest, so we had a leisurely dinner at the Vecchio. I had linguini con vongole, clams in white sauce, but Carmen packed away an appetizer of prosciutto e melon, a veal parm, a special salad of beets, chick peas and arugula and topped with a tortufo – an ice cream confection covered in dark chocolate with Neapolitan flavors. No wine, we were on duty.

We could hear the rave several blocks up on Lancaster and went in. Carmen assured me I looked alright, but that they no longer wore baseball hats backwards. She wore leggings and a peach tank top. We at least passed muster with the bouncer at the door collecting $20 each. Twenty bucks? Someone was making money, but it included flat beer from a poorly tapped keg. I could never understand why college kids never knew how to tap a keg properly. We each took a plastic cup and started in different directions. Even at 11:00 the place was only half full, but the line outside was swelling. I also never understood why the cops or the Liquor Control Board never shut these down.

We could see Avery up on the DJ stand, chattering away into the microphone. A few kids wandered up to him, so Carmen paced around and got a decent place to shoot on the DJ stand. Although I knew Carmen could take care of herself, I kept an eye on her as I scoped out the scene. I walked through clouds of pot smoke here and there. Kids sat and chatted at raised tables, or danced. A few made out in the corners.

I was much too old for this crowd so I hung in the corners and tried to sidle up to the DJ stand to take a few shots of the kids buying drugs. I also found Avery's competitor and took some snaps of him dealing. Carmen was, not surprisingly, very popular and asked to dance which hampered her sleuthing, but I did manage to catch a glimpse of her chatting up some of the people.

Avery eventually caught sight of me and managed to wave, fool that he was. Did he think we were making a social visit? Unfortunately, this drew the attention of his competitor who made his way over in my direction. He was a stocky fellow with some tattoos on his neck. He came up behind me.

"You a narc?" I turned to see him glaring at me.

"No." I wasn't happy about being made. "What's it to you?" "So this Andy, he's out on bail. You getting more shit on him?" "Why, you got something?"

"Maybe. Let's talk."

"Fair enough." We went out on to the sidewalk. "What have you got?" "Are you a narc or what?"

"No, I'm Andy's lawyer."

"Oh yeah, we heard. You went to make a plea deal and got turned down."

"How'd you hear that?"

"We got sources. So you want to give them something?"

"Who are you and what have you got?"

"I'm a Phantom. We used to be the Zombies, but we rebranded. Zombies was a bad image."

"Yeah, I get that."

"So why would the Phantoms give me shit I can use on the Dogs?"

"Come on counselor, you know better than that. We want to take over."

"Ok, I see, Good move. Do you want to talk?"

"Let's set up a meet. We got photos, sites, names, rap sheets. We done our homework."

"Sounds like a plan." He wrote out an address and a cell number on a napkin and handed it to me. I gave him my card.

"We got a house near Fifth and Olney. Can you make it at 6:00 tomorrow?"

I looked at the address. "I'll be there."

"Just you. No Andy."

"Got it. Who are you?"

"You already got my picture. Run it through the computer."

"See you at 6:00 p.m. then, on Olney."

I went back inside and collected Carmen, who was surrounded by a few guys. I waved her over. She frowned and reluctantly came to the door.

"I was having fun."

"Yeah, I'll bet. Did you get some good shots."

"I had to go to my second phone. I got at least fifty kids

buying from Andy and maybe 20 from his competitor. I got lots of the competitor.

"Great, we'll get them printed out and see who they are."

It was late. Too dangerous to walk to the el, so we Ubered to my car and I drove her home.

I got in late to the office the next morning, but Carmen was already downloading in living color shots of the kids. She sent a few shots of the competitor to our contact with the cops and got a reply. He was Horatio Lopez, a/k/a Flacco, a few minor drug possessions and a known member of the Phantoms.

La Cantina

As the office day came to a close, Carmen and I got ready to meet Officer Perez at La Cantina in the Northeast. I changed into jeans and an Eagles sweatshirt, always acceptable anywhere in Philly, and waited for Carmen outside the ladies room. What came out was a vision. Carmen had put on eye makeup and lashes with some blusher, and wore a shiny purple short (there is no word to describe how short) skirt and a tight bright pink top and stiletto heels.

"Whoa! Carmen, you're . . . you're . . ."

"Got it Pete. This is my battle gear. Don't tell the people in the office about this. My pushup bra already hurts. Let's get going." I have to say that she looked just wow. I know Officer Perez could not stand up to this.

Carmen giggled at my outfit. I had an Eagles tee shirt on. "Yo, Pete, you think that's Latino. No way. First, we don't follow football. It's either soccer or the Dodgers."

As we walked to the garage to pick up my car, she drew stares. I could only imagine what people thought about this middle-aged guy walking with a hot little Latina.

We got to La Cantina in the lower Northeast in a heavy Latino neighborhood. We split up and went in separately. I went to the bar and ordered a Tecate. She saw Perez and strutted up to him. He could not help himself saying "wow" either. She was definitely a hyacinth now.

I nursed the draft and stole a few glances at them, but they seemed to be having fun – laughing and giggling in Spanish. We were early so there were just a few scattered customers. Finally, they had a brief fight over the bill for drinks and a few plates of hors d'oeuvres as Carmen waved the firm's credit card at me. She shook hands with Perez and began to walk out. I followed her at a discrete distance. Over her shoulder, she said, "Got some good stuff Pete."

She walked to my car and got in when I clicked it open from a distance. "Ok, so what did you get? Maybe a date?"

"No! No! No! He knows my uncle from Willingboro and he's married. I'm no dummy, I don't do married."

"So what then?"

"Most of the cops in his district know this block of Apple. Where Avery got shot is at 3918, a known drug house. The second bloodspot is at 3926. This is a cathouse. The Penn boys and the locals go there to get laid. It's run by Aunt Ginnie, a large black woman, but she got a few bouncers there too.

"Apparently, these two houses pay off the local cops and the money gets funneled up to the lieutenants and captains. Perez is just a regular patrolman and doesn't do vice arrests or drug busts. He can just phone it in. Those are reserved for the vice and drug cops who take in the money. So the houses are protected. We weren't going to get any help from the detective or anyone on this. Perez, of course, wouldn't say this in court. It's a sure thing that Avery got moved around until he ended up at 3927 – the last of the blood spots. Someone moved the gun but not the shell casings there."

We were driving over to the duplex Carmen now owned and lived in with her aunt and cousin. I sat in silence, absorbing what she said. Then it came to me. We had to go to the cat house. Carmen, as usual was game for anything. So I turned the car back towards the city on Roosevelt Boulevard and went to Apple Street. Carmen had slipped out of her stilettos and put on her asic cross trainers and a grey sweatshirt. She was still dazzling in her eye makeup and blusher.

We pulled up to 3926 just after dark. I knew full well that a commercial venture of this sort enjoyed its confidentiality. Not from the cops. They each had a considerable investment in each other so they could trust the vice cops to keep the rest of the district in line. I also knew I was a suburban bred white boy lacking street smarts so I would need Carmen to weave through the rituals of this subculture. I could see four women in various lingerie fashions. As I walked into the room, one of the women gave my butt a healthy pinch. "Oh, nice tight cheeks." I turned to see a tall, black she-male person in a light blue bustier with exquisitely done makeup.

The transgender fellow giggled with delight. "So we got us a threesome. What you like honeybunch?" he said leering at Carmen.

"Back off, big boy." Carmen barked as he/she reached for her tight little tushy. "Who's in charge here?" The transgender fellow, looking very dejected, said, "Who wants to know?"

"Ben Franklin and two friends." A straight mercenary transaction. No hoo-hah. I originally guessed that the transgender fellow was the bouncer, but then two beefy fellows with no necks, shaved heads, and a half-lidded thousand yard stare came out of the back room. Since they might be able to grab my Carmen and swallow her in a single gulp, I decided it was my time to speak like a lawyer.

"Look, I don't want trouble. I'm a lawyer investigating the shooting a few days ago.

White guy, shot in the shoulder, up the block. I'll pay for

your time. Who's in charge here?" Everyone in the room turned as a heavy set middle-aged black woman in a something-

like-silk bathrobe came in. "I'm Aunt Ginnie. What can I do?"

"Ginnie, like short for Virginia?"

"You got a problem with that?" One of the no-necks challenged, but Ginnie waved him down.

"Fillmore, we got paying customers."

Turning to me, "Mr. . . . Mr. ?:

"Stern, Peter Stern." I handed her my card.

"Ah. A nice Jewish boy. We get lots of them. What do you like?"

"Information."

"How about little sparrow? How does she go?"

"No, just information for her too." I waved two hundred dollar bills and put them on the coffee table.

"About the guy shot up the block a few days ago."

"Oh, we don't know nothing."

"Yeah, yeah, I know. The cops kept you out of it and so will I. I just have to figure out what happened. And I think you know. Tell me what happened and I'm gone." Ginny looked around, picked up the two bills and put them into her ample bosom.

"Not much to tell. It was a nice night and we had been busy. We were sitting out front in beach chairs. Some of the girls were airing out their coochies. A white guy in an Audi drove up to the drug house yonder and got out. He started yelling something about "short bags." He musta bought this stuff from them and they had been giving him short weight. The guy we call "Pug Dog" come out and was yelling back. The white guy pulled out a gun and was waving it. Then a shot from some rifle came out of the second floor window, so we all ran inside. Then the white guy fell to his side and shot at Pug Dog and another guy came out the doorway with a bat and hit him up side the head. We all went back inside, closed up and turned out the lights. Then, two guys came out and dragged the white guy in front of our stoop along with the gun and shells. We don't need no police trouble, so my boys dragged him back up the street the other way along with the gun. Then we called 911 and went back inside and turned out the lights."

"Did your boys leave prints on the shells or the gun?"

"Are we stupid? Course not!"

"Do you know Ms. Jackson from up the block."

"Yeah, nice lady, she's a pre-school assistant. She shoulda stayed inside."

I nodded, looked at Carmen to see if she had any questions. She jerked her head to leave.

One of the women on the sofa dressed in a pink bra and silk panties said, "Where you going? You got forty-five minutes left. Or did you bring a sandwich from home? (glowering at Carmen).

"No, sorry, but no thanks."

Carmen and I left. Their story at least explained the three blood stains. But what did it mean for the case? I had to think this through.

First, we have Avery with a gunshot to his right shoulder lying on his back in front of 3927 with shell casings matching his gun and his gun nearby. He has gunshot residue on his hands. The car he drove was registered to his girlfriend, but had a pharmacopeia of drugs under the spare tire in the trunk.

All undeniable. All looked bad.

On the other hand, Ms. Jackson placed the argument and gun shots on the other side, the even numbered side of the street. By her testimony, Avery was the instigator of the action, waving his gun and arguing with the man inside a house. When he was shot, Avery could not plead self defense when he returned fire and put a man in the hospital. Without a knowledge of what the argument was about, Avery could have been attacking a perfectly innocent person at his residence. Even with the fact that the victim was a drug dealer, Avery had no right to threaten him or later shoot him. So no benefit to him there.

Meet with Phantoms

I had Angelina look up on Google the address I was given for the Phantoms. It was a Mexican restaurant with some parking. So I got out of my car and made the meet. As I shut my car door, two men came up to me quietly and asked me to get into a van. Actually, this gave me some confidence. This meant the gang I might do business with took precautions and were not just street thugs. They put a soft hood over my head, but we didn't go far, maybe only two or three blocks. I could feel myself lead into a damp area smelling of mold, probably a basement, and then up some wooden stairs. I was ushered to a seat and my hood came off. I found myself at an old dining room table surrounded by six chairs in a room with ancient floral wallpaper. The window shades had been pulled down.

Seated across from me were three men, including Flacco. "So, Mr. Stern, do you want to make a smart move?"

"I'm listening." A good lawyer always listens.

"You represent Avery Witherspoon. A Grade A asshole. He shot up his own supplier and is looking at major time." The man talking was a pleasant, somewhat beefy looking guy dressed in a red, collared golf shirt. He wasn't threatening and spoke softly. He wanted to negotiate. This was my milieu, business and deal making.

"No argument there!"

"The Dogs left the Apple Street house and scattered. They were all minor league guys anyhow. Nothing to cooperate with there."

"Ok so far."

"You had a meet with the DA and he told you this himself."

"I don't know how you heard this, but yes. That's where we are."

"So, we have lots of dirt on the Dogs and will let you have it. We want their territory and think giving the cops something to work on is better than a few shootouts. We want to play it smart and not bring too much attention to the operation."

"I can see that. Probably a good move."

"So we give you this stuff, have Avery get credit for it, and you get your plea deal."

"Ok, a few problems. One: the Dogs have paid me a hefty fee and told me not to have Avery cooperate. If he does, at the least I have to maybe give them back their very nice fee. At the worst, they know me and Avery. Two: Avery still goes to jail for some time and the Dogs get him in there. Three: the Dogs don't like me and will do something bad to me for cooperating against them."

"All good points. The first is your problem. You have to make all of your cooperation totally confidential. Avery doesn't testify and his plea in court is in chambers only. You announce that you have been fired as his attorney and let another one appear in your place.

"That can be done."

"Two: we reimburse any fee you have to return to the Dogs. Avery gets a witness protection deal and is sent somewhere in a prison under a different name."

"I've seen that done."

"As to you, we could give you a body guard, but I don't think you want that."

"No, I don't. That's all I need is some drug gang thug following me around while I conduct my practice."

"Ok, so no to that."

"Can I see what your information looks like. It has to be credible."

"Luis, bring me the box." Luis, a hefty fellow in a grimy tee shirt, brought over a Rolling Rock beer box. I could see stacks of photos with buys going on, and notes of the transactions.

There were shots of houses in the countryside with rental trucks parked and unloading boxes. The license plates were from Arkansas. The drivers and loaders were mostly Hispanic. Notes supplied their names, addresses and rap sheets. I perused most of the box. "Very impressive. You should hire yourself out to the DEA."

"No, we make more here." "I might have guessed that." "So, do we have a deal?"

"I have to ask my client, but it seems we have no other options."

"Here's a burn phone number. Give me a call if you can do it. We'll deliver a duplicate box to your office.

"I'll try to get Avery in on this."

"Fine. You've got two days." I rose, had my hood put on and was lead down the same wooden stairs, the basement and driven to my car.

Meet with Avery over Phantom Proffer

I was beginning to dread these conferences with Avery. He was, at least to me, a despicable human being. Often, a lawyer is not only required to associate with people he doesn't like, but also defend them. All the world then identifies the lawyer with his client. I am inundated with questions at cocktail parties, "How can you represent someone who is guilty?" The simple answer is that that is how our society works. So, when Avery ambled in at 11:00 for his 10:00 appointment, I was not thrilled. I was further disgusted when Aliyah/Alison came with him. I knew I was going to be asked a hundred dumb questions which belittled the effort I had made for him. My disgust for Aliyah was growing by the minute. After all, I was about to manufacture for him a proffer throwing his old gang, the Dogs, under the bus, which for no good reason, would benefit him by many years of hard prison time off his sentence. So Avery shambled in dressed in his usual black hard rock tour tee shirt and jeans. Alison, now Aliyah, was wearing short shorts and a tight tank top, the kind I had pulled off her many years before.

"So Avery, how are you doing?"

He glanced at Aliyah. "Not great." At least she had no visible bruises.

"I've been lucky enough to come into some valuable stuff on the Dogs which may save your sorry ass."

"Yeah, like what?"

"Lots of dirt. Where their drug houses are, who their people are, with pictures and rap sheets."

"Where did this come from?"

"Confidential. But a reliable source and credible with the DA."

"What did this cost?"

"More than you paid me." Why the hell was he interested in the expense? He himself had not paid me a dime.

"So, what do we do now?"

"Well, I draw up a summary for the DA and see what he would offer for the hard evidence. Then we bargain. I say you are a low level operative who will save some years in jail if you give them some useful information, but my dirt is very valuable. They look at it and hopefully decide the dope I give them is worth more than a few years extra in prison for a minor league criminal."

I have to say that, as I looked at him, I had to ask myself why I or anyone would want to help him. He was a useless ne'er do well, who hit women and had no prospects to lead a productive life. I had to keep this tone out of my voice.

"Can't I see the box of stuff you've got and know where you got it from."

"I promised it would be confidential." In reality, I knew this numbskull, if he got his hands on it, would figure out some way to screw up a plea deal and probably get him, and worse me, killed. No way was he getting the box.

Then, horror of horrors, Aliyah spoke up. "Is that the best you can do? Just a few years off his sentence." I mentally had to slap myself upside my head. What did she want with this useless piece of shit who only recently had beaten her up? And who was she to question the way I conducted business? So I just answered.

"Yes, that's the best. You do not understand that I got this marvelous windfall which I can use for a proffer. He is not going to walk or get probation. He shot a guy, he had drugs in his car, your car actually. You have to understand that the court will see him as a dealer to college kids of gateway drugs, not just to a bunch of losers on the street. He's looking at about 25 years. Maybe with this, he gets five years and has a life." I don't know why I was working so hard to sell this no-brainer deal to these numbskulls. He had gotten this magnificent gift out of the blue for no reason and without any effort on his part.

"What if we go to trial?" Again, Avery for some reason thought he could beat this mound of evidence.

"Yes, Peter. I thought you were supposed to be this hot shot trial guy." I decided not to take this bait for a major blowout and said, "I am good because I can evaluate situations. I have little doubt on this."

"Can we think about it?" she asked. Suddenly, she had a say in this. Of course, I was being paid by one of two drug gangs, not her, and now she felt she had a say.

"Fine, go think this through. Call me tomorrow." Avery got up and left. Aliyah lingered at the door. "Peter, why do you want Avery in prison? Is it because of me?"

I just shook my head. "No, it's not. He did this all by himself."

I was in a bad mood the rest of the day. What should have been greeted with cheers of triumph and pats on the back was looked on as if it was something the cat dragged in. And the arrogance, the arrogance, to believe that I was sending Avery to prison to what? To punish her, or worse, to get her back. I resolved to ignore this. I put on Mozart's Il Primo Concerto second movement and let its peaceful waves drift over me. When Angelina heard this, she knew not to disturb me.

Aliyah Response to Proffer

I had been putting off writing an important appellate brief in defense of a result I had gotten from a jury trial. I had read 487 pages of trial testimony, gotten opposing counsel's points for appeal, read his brief and was now composing my brief in opposition to his. My final step had been to compose in my head an outline of the points I wanted to include in my brief. I had written out my outline just as Mrs. Knecht in tenth grade had taught us and was grappling with how best to phrase each point. Angelina knocked on the door. "Peter, I got a visitor." I knew she would never disturb my thought process unless she had an important reason. Before I could reply, Alison/Aliyah had pushed past her and sat at one of the chairs in front of my desk.

"Peter, we have to talk." "Alison . . ."

"Aliyah . . ."

"I don't give a damn, Alison, I am busy and concentrating now, please leave me in peace." She was not a client, and her boyfriend was a difficult client. She did not deserve favored status.

I had in front of me the trial transcripts and four law books with sticky tabs on many pages. I had things carefully laid out in my mind. That was all gone.

"Look, I want to make sure you are doing everything you can for Andy."

"I am. There is no doubt in my mind that I am. And, what is more, you have no say in this. Last time I remember he got your car impounded and he beat you up. I saw the bruises and the photos to prove it."

"Are you somehow still mad about me breaking up with you when you went into the military? Do you want to deprive me of my boyfriend? Is this some way to get me back?"

"No, no and no. Your Avery is in a heap of trouble which he alone caused and the best he can do is cooperate and get a lesser sentence. It's as simple as that."

"So you don't want me back?"

"Not if you stuck needles in my eyes. You are . . ." I hesitated and should have stopped, but my good sense had left me. "You are a disaster. You have picked a total loser and you're getting older.   I can't see why you want to keep this schmuck. In my case, he is going to do some hefty stretch in jail and, as I recall, you are not good about waiting."

Oh no. She started to cry. Men are no good in this scene. So I handed her the box of tissues usually reserved for divorce cases and walked out of the office. Angelina, of course, was glued to the door. She smiled ruefully at me. After about five minutes, I went back in.

"Ok, so Alison . . ."

"Aliyah . . ."

"So what is Avery's decision? Cooperate or not."

"Yes, cooperate or whatever. Do what you think is best." The tears were gone. She got up icily and left.

My concentration on the brief was now long gone so I went for a walk and an ice cream cone.

Phantom Proffer

With the go ahead from Alison, I had Angelina number all the pages in the box and duplicate the photos and CDs. I called Ms. Liederkranz and told her I had a large proffer ready on the Dogs and arranged to come in. I asked that Lou Dawson attend as well. At 10:30, I wheeled the firm's hand truck over to the DA's office across from City Hall. When I got to the conference room, I was pleased to see Ms. Liederkranz and Lou Dawson waiting.

"So Peter, hope we can do business here today." Lou said jovially extending his hand. Ms. Liederkranz did too, but looked like she had just bit into a sour lemon. Was that her idea of a welcoming smile?

"So, I've got a ton of good information on the Dogs for your review." "No Avery today?" Lou asked.

"Avery wanted you to look at it and see if you needed him to testify later."   I was bluffing. There is no way Avery could substantiate any of this evidence. Only the Phantoms could. There was no way I would let Avery in the room to screw things up. I laid out the neatly marked piles of information, photos and CDs on the conference room table. "Please go through these. I think you'll find everything in order and that it will wipe out the Dogs. I'll go downstairs, get a coffee and come back in an hour. Let me know what you think then."

"Sure Peter. Let us go through all this."

I left and bypassed Starbucks. McDonald's had better and cheaper coffee. I sat and read the paper someone had left while I munched on a sausage biscuit. After an hour, I got a call on my cell from Lou.

"Peter, this is dynamite. Can I have the head of narcotics from the police come in and verify it?"

"Sure Lou."

"Can you come back tomorrow?"

"Sure Lou." I left. I was sure I had hooked a large fish. I went back to the office, returned some calls, signed some letters and waited for Lou's call. The longer I waited, the more intrigued they all would be by my materials.

It was 5:00 p.m. when Lou called. "Ok, Peter, we like it. It's authentic. How did you get it?"

"Lou, I'm not allowed to say. Do we have a deal?"

"Come on over and let's talk." I didn't have to be asked twice.

When I walked to the guards at the gate, they called me Mr. Stern, so I was getting increasing confidence we had a deal. I walked into their conference room, the contents of my box were strewn over the table. Captain Streher, the head of narcotics, was there with two other detectives. Lou extended his hand, and Ms. Liederkranz gave me another bitter lemon grimace which I now accepted was a smile.

"So, Captain Streher , is this the real deal?"

"Yes, Mr. Stern, great stuff. We could rip out the Dogs by the roots." "So Lou, what do we get for this?" He turned to Ms. Liederkranz.

In a voice which could curdle milk she said, "The total range of all the crimes we count, the maximum would be 45 years."

"Thank you, Ms. Liederkranz, I knew that."

"The guidelines recommend 27½ years, non-consecutive."

"Ah, we must be reading the same books." Another bitter lemon snark. This lady must cook children in her oven. I turned to Lou. "So what's your offer Lou? Remember, we get rid of a trial and this guy is a minor league dirtbag."

"Yes, Peter, calm down. We suggest five years max in Cressona or the new one near Graterford, eligible for parole after three. We remove the violent tag so he can be a trustee with good behavior."

It was a good deal, better than he deserved. But a lawyer always bargains. "How about four years, and all the above, but parole eligibility after two years."

"Wait here, Peter." I waited while they left to huddle. They already had all my stuff, so the cat was out of the bag. They must also know Avery was taking a risk giving this stuff up, but after this, I had nothing to bargain with.

They walked in, grim-faced. "No, Peter, the deal we offered is the deal." I shrugged. "I'll tell my client, Lou. Nice doing business with you." I went home that night feeling I had done a major work for that no-account Avery. Five years in soft time with early parole was a godsend. I went back to the office and called Avery, but got Alison.

"Alison, let me speak to Avery." "Peter, it's Aliyah and Andy." "Let me speak to them too."

Avery got on another phone. "Peter what is it?"

"I think you got really lucky. It's non-negotiable, but you get a 2½ to five year sentence soft time. They remove the violent tag. This means you are not labeled a violent inmate and can, with good behavior, become a trustee after one year. Soft time means Cremona, which usually houses older or sick men, or the new Graterford site, about a 45 minute drive from Philadelphia."

There is silence. Alison spoke up. "You mean he's gone for 2½ years?"

"To be honest, it might be more. Parole is no longer automatic, he has to earn it."

"So when could he get out?"

"I'm guessing maybe 3, 3½ years."

"Mr. Stern," now Avery was calling me Mr. Stern. "I can't do time. I'll go crazy."

"Andy, I can't do any better. You did some bad things. You're getting a major gift with the proffer I gave them."

Alison spoke up. (Never one to stand by her man.) "I don't like it."

"Look, Andy, Aliyah, it is the best I can do."

"Do you mind if we get a second opinion?"

"Knock yourself out." I hung up. I was hungry and ready for dinner at home. I drove grumbling to myself for not being appreciated.

Acceptance of Plea

It wasn't long before Avery and Alison ambled into the office without an appointment. When the receptionist buzzed me that they were there, I had half a mind to hide in the men's room and tell them to get an appointment next time, but that would just prolong our little dance. So I let them in, but made them wait.

Finally, I called them back with Angelina in attendance. They sat looking unhappy. "So, whom do I deliver your file to Avery? Who is your next lawyer?"

"What? No . . . no . . . you keep it."

"So what was this second opinion."

"He said I was lucky. He said you were doing us a favor because Aliyah was your ex."

"Ah, so he had the whole story. What did he charge you?"

"Five hundred in cash."

"Well, that's more than you've paid me."

"Yeah, well, so what do we do now?"

"Schedule a plea in chambers so your deal does not become public and neither me nor you gets killed."

"When is that?"

"Soon. When would you like it, sooner or later? This judge will be accommodating."

"Oh, later."

"So about two weeks to settle your affairs."

"Wow, just two weeks."

"With the deal done, the DA won't wait too long."

"If that's what it has to be." They left. Angelina gave me a grimace and an eye roll.

"Peter, there's a package for you up front. You have to sign."

I went up front. There was a UPS box. I had a feeling what it was, so I got Laura and Angelina to come to the small conference room.

As I was opening it, they both came in to see stacks of 100's on the table. Laura was aghast. "Peter, what is this, more drug gang payoffs."

"Yes, Laura. Not exactly my choice, but that's the way they do business. So put this in the safe for now."

"As we counted and put the stacks back in the box, Laura was holding them at arms' length with extended fingers, pinkies up. "I swear Peter, bring in some corporate clients."

"Yes, I get it, Laura. So should I scatter this on Market Street?"

"No. No, we'll make payroll this week."

Angelina came in and sat. "So what one you gonna do. One side pays you not to cooperate, one side pays you to cooperate. What'll you do?"

"Why, of course, ask Digby." And that's what I did.

DEA Visit

The office was mercifully quiet for a few days. Stacks of paper started to disappear from my desk and credenza. Angelina was chirping happy songs as she pecked away at her keyboard. Only Carmen was bored. She was given the usual paralegal tasks of sorting, or filing, or researching on the internet. But things were quiet. I had briefed Digby on the whole plea arrangement and he was in agreement. Our client, our prime responsibility, had been more than well served. We had a double fee in the safe. Allison got her car back. And the City of Philadelphia was going to be rid of one large drug gang near the Penn-Drexel campus. Yes, Digby saw it as a win-win-win as did I. I celebrated by leaving early to watch my daughter in a soccer game. She was built like my wife, petite but athletic.

Then about 11:00 a.m., I could hear a hubbub in the office. I could hear Angelina say, "Uh-oh, here comes trouble."

Three men and a woman came to my door escorted by the receptionist who said, "I'm sorry, they insisted on going right in."

"That's alright, Sherry. Gentlemen, and lady, please come in." Lou Dawson was the first in and three others followed. I only had two chairs, so the lady and one of the men took them. It was clear Lou was not in charge, but I turned to Lou. "What's this about?"

The older man in the chair handed me a card and said, "Albert Gruchacz, DEA Section Chief." He was followed by "Anna Marie O'Leary, Intelligence Operations," and "Harry Cipollone, DEA Special Agent."

"Is there a problem?"

"Yes, Mr. Stern, there is." Albert Gruchacz blurted. "Where did you get the materials in the box you proffered to Mr. Dawson?"

I didn't like his attitude and I wasn't about to upset the apple cart, so I used one of my favorite excuses. "You are aware of attorney-client privilege, aren't you?"

Law enforcement hates that phrase almost as much as Doctor-Patient, but Gruchacz blundered ahead. "You have compromised a very large operation we are mounting in West Philadelphia. Some of our best informants have been picked up and are being squeezed for information."

"Ah ha! So the Philadelphia narcotics people have started to act on the stuff I gave them and those people were DEA informants."

"Yes. We don't like butting heads with the Philly cops."

"I can see that. Why don't you cooperate better with them?" I knew this was an unpopular question. He would never admit that they didn't trust the Philly narco cops.

"Why do you come to me?"

"If someone in the DEA leaked this information to you, we want to know."

"Have you looked at the information? Is it something that looks like it came from your files?"

"Frankly no, but it came from somewhere. And we would like to know where."

"If you knew, would you still let the Philly cops arrest your own informants among the Dogs?"

"We'd have to see about that."

"More important, this information was supposed to be confidential. If it gets out that we cooperated as part of a plea deal, then Avery and I are in deep trouble with the Dogs."

"That may be so."

"So why would I expose my client and myself to this danger?"

"It may impact on your plea deal." I didn't like the sound of that. I turned to Lou. "Is this true, Lou?" You would back out on your deal?" I was not happy.

"Now Peter, don't get wound up. They just want to know some of the facts."

"Do we still have a deal?" Lou didn't answer. "I'd take this to court. Do you want the City to know the DA's office does not stand behind its plea deals, especially after they get all the information. I will make this public. And I will make it obvious that the DEA is blundering into narcotics enforcement by not coordinating with the Philly cops because they don't trust them." By now I was shouting.

Gruchacz did not like the sound of this, nor did Lou. They went out into the hallway and huddled. After a few minutes, Gruchacz returned. "Mr. Stern, you haven't heard the last of this."

I was about to shout, "Don't let the door hit you in the ass on the way out." Maybe I had grown up, maybe not.

As they walked out, Angelina grinned. "Oops, I left the intercom on. I hope you're not mad. I was right next to the answering machine and, oops, it may have recorded the whole thing.

"Angelina, you are a naughty girl." I grinned. My personal

she-wolf was not napping.

I was not happy with Lou sounding iffy on our deal. There are lots of outs in the plea agreement including committing new crimes, or falsely implicating someone. Then there are lots of other restrictions: traveling out of state or some minor infractions. The life's blood of big city DA's office though are plea deals. Almost 90% of arrests result in pleas and save the court huge amounts of time and effort. Judges usually accept the deals DA's have made so the whole court system runs smoothly. Every once in a while some judge gets a bug up his ass and decides to defy the DA's office for being too soft, but this is rare; but the DA must be trustworthy or he gets no deals.

But I could feel problems cropping up. Avery was a squirrelly character, and even Alison was capable of doing something to jeopardize the deal. The sooner I put this baby to bed, the better. I called up the Court Administrator to move the date of the plea hearing up.

Post Gruchacz

I did not like Gruchacz's tone. It had the rumblings of Polish pogroms. I could hear horses coursing up to my little town ready to pillage and plunder. It was an ancestral thing I just have heard; he was a bully and I don't like being bullied.

So, as I walked out to the street from my home, I heard a rustling in the bushes. Several large hooded men and a short stocky black man came rushing toward me with a large bag. In the few seconds before I could react I recognized Pug Dog. I was struck a few times in the ribs as they slid the bag down over me and I was lifted off the ground. I felt my side. It was sore but bearable. They had not wanted to kill me. This must be some retaliation for what they thought was Avery's cooperation. How they heard about this I don't know. Obviously, Lou and Ms. Liederkranz knew and the Captain of the Philly narco cops, but it leaked somehow to the Dogs. Could this be Gruchacz? The Phantoms certainly didn't do it. But it was somewhat late in the game, cat was already out of the bag, and the Dogs were being rounded up as we spoke. I was frog marched to a van and thrown to the floor. It was definitely a time to be scared, but I had to keep my cool. I was about to meet some higher-ups for questioning. The van rumbled along for maybe a half hour and bounced up some driveway and into a garage. The van stopped and I slid off the back end to an upright position. I could smell damp mold, a cellar, then up some wooden stairs, definitely a residence, and onto a wooden floor. At some point, I was told to sit. I felt with my hands for a chair and felt a metal kitchen dinette chair. My hood was left on. I was put in plastic hand cuffs.

"So, Stern, you been bad, very bad." I recognized the voice from before. The no cooperation guy with the words dragged out. I figured it was best to let him come to the point after he had made his macho pseudo German interrogator act. "Andy was not supposed to cooperate (that word again). He did. We gave you $35,000 for a trial, but we got a plea."

"Let me explain something to you. A lawyer's first and only loyalty is to his client. If you pay my fee, I only represent him, not me. If I don't do that, I lose my license and he gets to sue me for big bucks.

"He always has the right to ignore me and my advice. He hasn't really listened to me since I started to represent him. I don't know what he may have done. I can tell you, I was never present when he discussed anything about a plea with the DA." I am not particularly proud of these lies by omission, but I was after all kidnapped and looking at some kind of violence. So a half truth it was.

"Where is Andy now?" This threw me for a loop. Obviously, Andy had gone into hiding or fled. This might be a violation of his bail or his plea deal. I wasn't going to tell them that.

"I don't know. He lives with either his girl friend or his mother."

"We checked both. We got blank looks from both places. His girl friend still has her car."

"If that's the case, I don't know where he is. So what's happened so far with the Dogs."

"They been made. 14 street guys and two messengers."

"Where are they now?"

"We don't know. The cops got them on ice and are interrogating the hell out of them. Some guys got families or records. They may flip."

"Who could have done this?"

"No Sabe, we don't know. The DEA people say they don't know. We gave them lots of information. But they ain't talking."

"So the Dogs are being wrapped up. Why don't you merge with the Phantoms?" This was my corporate lawyer I was channeling.

"Nah. We're black, they're Hispanic. We won't mix."

I shrugged. I had nothing more. They hoisted me to my feet and led me up some wooden stairs, down a short wooden hallway and sat me down on a desk chair.

The room was dark and quiet. I could see my feet under the hood and on the floor were several piles of mail. The address was 716 Nedro. So I knew where I was. I heard some whispering to my left.

"Is someone there?"

"Who's that? Is that you, Peter?" Oh no, they had kidnapped Alison too. That's all I needed. More baggage.

"So what happened to you?"

"This morning, they were banging on my door and broke in. I was in a short nightie. They grabbed me. They squeezed my boobs and felt my pussy. I screamed. I am in a small apartment house so they stopped. Then, they let me get dressed and put this hood on me. Sometimes they bring me a sandwich and a coke."

"What did they want?" "Where Andy was." "Did you know?"

"No, skipped a few days ago after he heard he had to do time."

"So, you have no idea where he is?"

"No, we had a big fight before he left."

"Did he hit you again?"

"No. Are you getting off on that?"

"No. No, do you know where to find him?

"Not really. He has friends down south. I never met them. I don't know where they live. They are kind of wealthy."

"Good, the less you know the better."

"So, what do we do?"

"Did they take your cell phone?"

"Yes."

"Maybe, they can trace us from that."

"So what do we do now? Shall I tell you how they grabbed my boobs and sucked my nipples, or maybe fingered my pussy?"

"Jees, Alison, you are a piece of work!"

"You used to like to hear about it. Don't you like it any more?"

"I'm not into violence against women."

"Yes, you were always a gentle lover."

"Do we need to talk about this? It was years ago."

"I remember that rainy day at the Schwenksville Folk Festival when we went in the tent. One window was open and you took me from behind. I made so much noise, I had to pretend I was barking."

"Alison, please! You left me years ago when I went into the military."

"Oh, Peter, you came back home that one weekend with that shaved head and your uniform. You looked so schmucky."

"I didn't have a choice. I wasn't going to run like other guys."

"Most of my friends went to Canada."

"Exactly. I felt I had a duty to my country."

"Yeah. And fight in Vietnam?"

"I didn't know all that at the time."

"Oh, Peter, you were such a boy scout."

"I guess so."

"All the other guys had long hair to their shoulders and tie-dyed shirts. And you, in that uniform."

"I never wore the uniform in Philly."

"No, but when I came down to look at the base, it was disgusting. All those know- nothing peasant girls. I couldn't live with them."

"So you fucked around with everyone else?"

"I guess so. I was feeling lonely."

"So you've had a good life and hooked up with Avery. He's very handsome."

"Oh shut up. I'm almost forty. He's good to me."

"Yeah, I saw the black eye."

"Don't forget the bruise on my left boob."

"So where is he?"

"Gone, with my kitchen money."

"Not your car."

"No, not my car. Thank you very much."

"So he's violated his bail conditions and his guilty plea agreement."

"What's that mean?"

"All bets are off. The court can sentence him up to 25 or 30 years."

"He's so good looking, he'll be somebody's girl friend in no time."

"Or everybody's girl friend."

"So, Peter, won't you come see me sometimes."

"Alison, you are a disaster. I can see that is a bad idea."

"So what do we do now?"

"Alison, I've been thinking."

"Ok, Peter, it's what you do best."

"Yeah, yeah. Your hands are behind you in those handcuffs, right?"

"Yes."

"So, I'm going to crawl on my hands and knees to your rear."

"Be still my heart."

"Alison, pay attention. When you can feel my hood, I want you to grab it and I will try to back out of it. Got it?"

"Yeah, I got it."

"Then, I'll pull your hood off. You will get on your knees in front of me."

"Too easy, Peter, give me a hard one. Oops, I mean."

"Alison, please pay attention."

"Yeah, so I'm on my knees and you pull my hood off."

"Good. Then we try to get out of here."

I went to my knees as quietly as I could and knee-walked over to where I heard Alison's voice. "Alison, speak up so I can find you."

"Marco . . . Marco"

"Very good." I found myself butting my head against her chair. I could feel her find the top of my hood. "Ok, now hold tight." I backed up and my hood slid up my torso and over my head. I could walk to the front of Alison and grasp her hood. "Ok, Alison, on your knees." She stood and kneeled down as the hood fell to one side. Ok, so we could see, but we were still handcuffed in plastic handcuffs. I tiptoed around the room, and went over to the window which had newspaper taped over it. I pulled off the newspaper. I was looking into the rear alleyway which ran the entire block. Below us, just one story down was a landing area with a staircase leading out to the alleyway.

"Alison, come here, can you jump onto that landing?"

"One story huh! With no hands. Ooo! No good. Can you go first and kind of catch me."

"Yeah, I can do that." There was a trash can on the landing giving just three feet square to land in. It had to be done. By now, it was still light out. I pulled the window up and put one foot outside and looked around to see if the coast was clear. I flexed my knees and dropped ten feet to the landing. Because my knees were flexed, I hardly made any noise.

Alison followed me out the window. I moved the trash can aside giving her more landing room.   I was happy to see she was wearing jeans and sneakers. She slid off the window ledge and I caught her on the way down.

My hands were behind me, so she fell up against me with a big smile. "I want a kiss cause I earned it."

"Oh, Alison, not now!"

"One kiss or I'm not moving." I kissed her and got a full open mouth.

"Ok, you idiot, follow me." We scampered down the alleyway with our hands behind us. About two blocks up was a Wawa, so we walked to the sandwich counter. I spoke to the chief sandwich maker, a large jolly black woman, "Please cut off these handcuffs. There's a $20 in it for you."

Bam! The handcuffs were cut. "What have you two been doing?" she asked with raised eyebrows and a leer.

"Don't ask. Just look at the smile on his face." Alison said rubbing her wrists. That drew a hearty chuckle. I gave her a $20.

"Now we have to borrow a phone." There was a Chinese restaurant around the corner.

We went in. It was near dinner time.

"So, can I make a call on your phone?" He nodded and pointed at the landline for receiving takeout orders. "I need to call Uber, charge it to your phone."

I managed to get one of the restaurant patrons to get me an Uber. I paid them for the charge. So, Alison and I drove back to her apartment. She started making small talk and was chattering nervously. I had to say, "Alison, please let me think. I don't know how the Dogs got the information that Avery may have cooperated. That is important. What we gave the DA was confidential, and we have not had a plea hearing yet, so there was a leak."

"Ok, so who?"

"I'm thinking not the Philly narcotics Captain. He's making arrests and looking good. Did the Dogs figure it out because they were being rounded up. Or maybe Gruchacz, I never liked him."

"So how do you figure it out?"

"First I talk to Lou Dawson. He's supposed to be a trustworthy guy. Now where is Avery?"

"You mean Andy?" "Ok, Andy."

"I don't know. Maybe down south like I said."

"That's bad for him. He has lost the whole benefit of the deal. And you've lost your bail money."

"You mean they keep $10,000 if he doesn't show."

"That's what bail means. You put up 10% of $100,000. They keep that if he doesn't show. You get it back if he shows. That's how it works."

"Oh, not good. That's my father's money. He will be pissed. He never liked Andy anyway. He liked you."

"First, the Dogs put up the money, not you. I liked your father too. Nice guy."

"I liked you too."

"Yeah, so I can tell."

"Now, Peter, that's in the past." Fortunately, silence prevailed after that. So I could go over in my mind how the Dogs got word of our cooperation.

Meet with Dawson

The next day, I camped out at the door to the DA's office since admission was strictly limited even after I had gone through the metal detector. Shortly after 9:00 Lou appeared.

"Peter, what are you doing here?"

"Lou, we have to talk. Not here."

"Ok, come on in." He was waved through with me in tow. He went to his office and pulled the shades. "So, what's up."

"Lou, Aliyah and I were kidnapped by the Dog gang yesterday. We escaped yesterday.. They seem to know Avery was cooperating and couldn't find him, so they went after Aliyah, his girlfriend, and me. So I figure there's a leak. That cooperation was supposed to be confidential."

"I have a problem too. Avery is not reporting in to his bail supervisor. He seems to have skipped."

"Ok, you help me; I help you."

"Kidnapping is a serious crime. So let's see about that." "Where were you taken to?"

"716 Nedro."

"How do you know that?"

"I saw some mail on the floor. I can ID the house."

"So it was a residence.,"

"Yes."

"Did they take your cell phones?"

"Yes. I guess they want to see if we have been in contact with Avery."

"Yeah. Probably. So hold on a second." He picked up the phone and said, "Get me Communications." "If they have the phones, we can tell where they are. In the meantime, I will alert SWAT to take them down if we can find them."

"Wow? I'm impressed." I gave him my cell number and Aliyah's and he relayed it to Communications.

"So what else?"

"Someone leaked the fact that there was cooperation against the Dogs by Avery."

"Uh-huh. So not me, probably not Martha. I guess not Captain Streher of the city narc squad. Maybe DEA."

"That's what I thought. Could it be Gruchaz?" "First, I'll call Martha."

"Who is Martha?"

"Ms. Liederkranz." He buzzed an intercom button. "Martha, can you come up to my office?"

Ms. Liederkranz arrived in a light gray pantsuit and orange blouse with tan Hush Puppies.

She brought in a rolling case with the case files. "Yes, Lou."

"Martha, Mr. Stern here and Avery's girlfriend were kidnapped by the Dogs to find out about this cooperation. They wanted to find Avery. Do you have any thoughts on this?"

She stared into space. "I can't figure the Philly cops, they're already making arrests.

This was a big windfall for them." "So, Gruchaz?"

"I can't believe a DEA agent would do that." "Ok, you think about it."

By now, Communications had called Lou back and confirmed

that our cell phones were still at 716 Nedro. Lou called SWAT. They had assembled a squad of four. They would be by to pick up Lou in five minutes.

"Lou, I want to go."

"Mmm . . . not good Peter."

"I can ID these guys."

"Ok, you asked. Put on a vest." We ran to the front of the building. Lou handed me a vest which I put on. We got in the sedan and a dark green van followed us.

"Oh, Lou, when we get there, they also beat me up around the ribs and they sexually assaulted Aliyah."

"Ok, Agg Assault and a whole list of sex crimes. I'll take care of that if we get them"

We went down Broad Street with sirens on to Nedro, going through the lights. We pulled up to 716 Nedro.

"Peter, you stay in the car. Do not move!" Lou got out a silver pistol and stayed in the roadway behind the car. The SWAT team split up, some to the front, some to the rear. I heard a thumping on the door and someone shouting "Police". Another thumping and more shouting.

Nothing. The men in the front brought a large iron cylinder with handles and swung it at the door. The door popped open. I could hear an argument from inside. Then, one of the swat cops waved us up.

On the floor, on their bellies in the front room, handcuffed behind their backs were three men, all grumbling noisily. As I walked in the door, I recognized Pug Dog immediately.

"This isn't your day, Pug Dog. Where's my phone?" He shrugged. So I started a search. It wasn't hard. There were two phones. I recognized mine right away. I knew fingerprints were an issue, so I just pointed and one of the cops got out a bag. The second phone had a pink plastic cover. This was bagged as well.

One of the guys on the floor said. "What about our deal?"

"It's a little late for that, don't you think. Lou, I'll explain all this later."

"Ok, men, take them in." The men were hoisted to their feet and put face down in the rear of the van. They would take the men to Seventh and Vine for an arraignment. Lou and I went back to Center City.

"Ok, so now. What is this deal?"

"The Dogs told me they wanted no cooperation. We never agreed, but they sent a large container of money in cash to my office.   I knew there was no way Avery had a prayer in front of a jury. My advice had always been to cooperate. So we left the money in the office safe. Finally, I was convinced that the Dogs were out to save themselves and he would spend 25 years in jail. Eventually, Avery agreed. So we cooperated. Regardless of who pays the fee, I always must represent only the client."

"True enough."

"So where did all the cooperation material come from." "Sorry, Lou, can't say."

"You know, I have to look at the phones and see what you've been doing. "But there may be attorney-client communications on there."

"Not for Aliyah."

"True. But I don't use my cell much. Let me think about what I may have done. You can keep the phone. Can I limit the dates?

"I guess so. When did you first have a contact with Avery?"

"The day he was shot. But I think his mother called into the office on the landline. So, whenever that was."

"Fair enough. Avery's shooting to present. You get to review it first in my office before you object on attorney-client privilege grounds."

"Fair enough." I could only guess what Alison had on her phone.

I also could only guess how well Avery could cover his tracks. Law enforcement has many ways of tracing bail jumpers.

As we sat talking, I could see into Ms. Liederkranz's case files. There was a cell phone in an evidence bag and a Search Warrant receipt.

"Ms. Liederkranz, is that Avery Witherspoon's cell phone?"

"Yes."

"Weren't you supposed to get into it and transcribe the conversations?"

"Yes, but as the case against him got to be so overwhelming, I decided we didn't need it."

"But you got a search warrant for it, didn't you?"

"Yes, we do that right away."

"Lou, there may be valuable stuff on there. Can I see it?"

"I don't know. It's still evidence."

"But I should be able to see it too."

"That's true. It costs about $500 to transcribe about 100 pages."

"I'll pay it. Get it done."

"How far back?"

"Let's go 100 pages and see what happens."

"Fine. Ms. Liederkranz, please." She left rolling her files behind her. I left and called Alison.

"Alison,"

"Peter, it's Aliyah I told you."

"Ok, Aliyah. I'm about to look into what's on Avery's phone. Is there anything I'm going to find that I shouldn't."

"I don't know Peter. There was a lot of things I didn't know."
"Ok. How are you feeling?"

"Alright. I finally got my door fixed after the break in."

"Good. Well, see you."

"Bye Peter."

ID's and Statements in DA's Office

Alison and I had to return to the DA's office to make formal statements and officially ID those Dogs who were arrested. Captain Streher and his lieutenant in charge of the Dogs takedown were present.

I retold how I had been taken prisoner after being roughed up at my house. I retold the trip in the van, the climb of the stairs to be interrogated with a hood on. The conversation we had and my being parked on the second floor with Alison. The lieutenant took careful notes and asked a few questions for clarification. I described our escape out the window onto the landing and the handcuff removal and Uber call. If this matter became seriously contested, each point that corroborated my story might have to be verified. I ID'd Pug Dog and the man who had approached me earlier about "no cooperation." It turned out he was one of the men we arrested at 716 Nedro.

Aliyah/Alison asked that I be present as she told her story. Although I was not her attorney, they permitted me to remain. She told her story about her relationship with Avery, then her kidnapping. As she was describing the early morning break in at her apartment, she described her breasts being fondled and her pussy being grabbed. The lieutenant, in a lowered somewhat hesitant tone, asked, "Did his finger penetrate you?"

"You mean did he stick his finger up my vagina?"

"Yes, ma'am."

"Yes, he did."

She turned to me and whispered, "I was going to give him a half hour to stop."

I rasped back, "Alison, please take this seriously." She pulled her long face and continued her story, the hood, the ride in the van, the interrogation, the escape. The lieutenant dutifully took voluminous notes. Then, he got out piles of photos and asked her to ID her attackers.

She had a decent view of them when they first came in the apartment and readily ID'd all three from three large photo arrays. Finally, we were done. Alison had taken a half day off from work. "So, Peter, aren't you going to spring for lunch." Reluctantly, I took her in full view of the Center City crowd to my usual deli.

"Alison . . ."

"Aliyah."

"Ok, Aliyah, why do you keep playing these games. I told you I'm happily married, I have two kids, a mortgage, a van, and I don't need trouble from you."

"Who says I'm trouble? I saw that petite little ballet person, no makeup, and a tight tush in black jeans. She'll never know."

"Yes, she will and so will I."

"Didn't that part about the guy penetrating me get you a little stirred up?"

"I have to admit I was, but I don't think like you. You like guys like Avery."

"Oh, he can be exciting."

"And you're not too loyal or dependable."

"Oh, you're still mad at me."

"Well, yeah. You deserted me at my weakest point."

"So, I'm sorry."

"Alright. It's in the past. I survived."

"And did well."

"I guess so!"

"So, Alison . . ."

"Aliyah."

"Aliyah, let's leave it at that, in the past."

"Alright. So what do I do now. Avery has taken off."

"Oh, he'll be caught. There are too many ways you pop up on some government computer."

"And he'll do major time now."

"Yeah, our plea deal is in the dumper. The cops got a ton of information and Avery didn't stay around to get the benefit of a lucky windfall. Did he take anything from you?"

"No car this time, just about $40 in kitchen money."

"I wonder how he got his DJ equipment and all his sound stuff."

"All that is gone from my apartment. I guess he got a truck or a van some place." We finished our sandwiches and shook hands.

Review of Avery's Phone Transcript

When I got back to the office, I asked Angelina and Carmen to come to the small conference room to review the transcript of Avery's phone messages. They contained numbers he called without more, as well as all of his text messages and they went back a year in time before the night he was shot on Apple Street.   I divided the pages up and gave each of them a pile of sticky notes and few highlighter pens.

We sat and started to flip through the pages. It was Carmen, reviewing the earliest pages, that noticed a similarity of numbers being called. We already had Alison's number, so any other frequently repeated calls would draw attention. We also had the Dogs' number from Apple Street. They were eliminated. Then a series of numbers cropped up.   Before we went further, we did a reverse number search and found it went to a blocked number. The police could unblock the number, but we couldn't, so we made a note of this.

Then there were texts to that number. "need 5k", "CU at 2", "need 5K", "Dogs ask", "Any X?" The more we found these messages, the more they sounded like drug talk. Of course, Avery was a drug dealer, but then who was he messaging and calling at this number?

We finished the 100 pages and neatly placed them in a file with sticky notes. The calls were usually on Fridays or Sundays. Since Avery's raves were on Fridays and Saturdays, they may have had something to do with the raves. Too much coincidence. Time to call Lou to get the reverse number. Carmen and Angelina listened in. They were not about to miss this.

"Lou, how ya doin'? I got a few questions on these transcripts."

"Ok, shoot."

"Some go to blocked cell numbers. Can you do a reverse search for me?"

"Sure, what were the messages about?"

"Could be drug talk."

"No problem. I'll call you right back."

After we hung up, Carmen said, "I think some of these numbers go directly to the Fifth Squad." She was referring to the narcotics cops in detective headquarters at 55th and Pine.

"That's not good. Why is Avery speaking to the narco cops?"

"Maybe he has to pay them off."

"Could be, but the Dogs would take care of that. They wouldn't want a low level dealer doing that. Let's see what Dawson comes up with."

It wasn't long. "Yo, Peter, I got the number. It's a private cell phone billed to Meg Keely in the northeast.

"Any idea who this Meg Keely is?"

"That's Lieutenant Keely's daughter. She's six years old. Lieutenant Keely is the head of the narcotics cops in the 39th District. Why is Avery calling him? Can I see his messages?"

"Lou, if the cops are involved, I would just as soon keep this really confidential. I don't want to discuss this in your office. Can you get someone from Internal Affairs to come with you to my office?

"Good idea, Peter, I'll be on it."

I handed Lou an envelope with five $100 bills in it out of the $35,000 I had been given by the Phantoms. He signed a receipt and handed over a file. "Peter, the $500 bought you 100 pages, so I put them all in the file. Let me know if you come up with anything."

While we waited for Dawson to assemble some brass from the Internal Affairs Division, Angelina and Carmen stayed in the conference room sorting out phone numbers and text messages. The questionable drug numbers were highlighted in red. But I could hear some giggling as Angelina and Carmen sorted out something else. I stuck my head in, "So what's this buzz I hear?"

"Peter, I'm sure we got a girlfriend number and a few explicit texts. We got a new blue highlighter for them."

I looked at their sheets. Large blue streaks here and there.

"We did a reverse number search and got a Cheryl Czpanski. She lives in the northeast, owns a van and has a thing for Avery. Her Facebook page has lots of shots of a pretty blond girl, goes to Drexel. Our Avery was cheating on your Alison."

I looked over what they got. I had Angelina call her number on the pretext of a sales call for windows. A cheery voice answered.

"Oh, I don't need windows. I live in a dorm." Drexel had a Cheryl Czpanski enrolled. Yes, definitely some side action for our boy Avery. I knew this was a problem. We had to bring in Alison to help ID some of the numbers. She would soon learn of Cheryl and I did not want to face the fallout.

I got a call back from Lou. "Peter, I got Lt. Mehle of Internal Affairs. He wants to meet at 2:00 this afternoon. OK by you?"

"Good. See you then."

I called Alison. "So, Aliyah, we opened up Avery's cell phone and have a lot of calls and texts. I was hoping you could identify some of the numbers."

"Why do you want me for this?"

"So we can locate him."

"But doesn't that mean the cops will find him and send him to jail, right?"

"Yes, probably."

"So, I won't help. I don't want him in jail Peter."

"Ok, I get it."

Lt. Mehle of the Internal Affairs Division came with a reputation that preceded him. He was known as "Twang" because he was such a straight arrow. Internal Affairs (IA) officers in general are reviled throughout the rest of the police department because their mission is to go after dirty cops. When a cop is caught doing something, IA steps in to develop the case. Unfortunately, the process usually finds the cop did something wrong and frequently reinstates him with full back pay after a lengthy vacation. The process goes through an arbitrator selected jointly by the Fraternal Order of Police and the Police Commissioner. Even though cops survive this process, they are tainted for promotion and most commanders don't want them in their divisions. But Lt. Mehle never had any friends in the department even though he was a competent and thorough investigator. He came in precisely at 2:00 p.m. with a deputy. Angelina escorted him into the conference room and Carmen and I joined him. He, of course, refused coffee or a soda because he would never accept anything from a civilian and that was us.

I briefed him on the entire shooting which brought Avery into police custody, the procedural status of the case, the whole proffer deal, my kidnapping, the ongoing action against the "who let the Dogs out?" gang, Avery's disappearance, and so on.

He and his deputy were each taking notes and asking clarifying questions. As I went, I slid documents across the table to support our position. He nodded and let out an occasional, "Hmm!"

"So he's a DJ at a Lancaster Avenue rave and he sells dope to college kids. He's already proffered a whole boxful of materials on the Dogs. But you don't want to say who gave you this or how Avery got it."

"True."

"I'm going to need to know that."

"Will this be confidential? I'm concerned that if it leaks how we got this, it may endanger us or compromise the investigation."

"You know IA plays its cards close to the vest."

"True. Ok. The Phantoms gave it to me. They knew it would help me got a better sentence for Avery and it would hurt their competitors, the Dogs."

"That's pretty obvious. So, we've got two actors in West Philly, the Dogs and the Phantoms."

"Yes."

"Did Avery have anything to do with the Phantoms or did the Phantoms give this box directly to you?"

"No, they gave it directly to me. Avery never saw it, but he knew I was giving it to the DA on his behalf."

"So, the Phantoms get rid of a competitor and Avery gets his deal."

"Exactly."

"But Avery disappears and voids the entire deal so he is still looking at major time."

"Do you know where he got his drugs to sell while he was out on bail and couldn't get supplied by the Dogs."

"He says he had a stash saved up."

"So he sold at how many raves in the meantime?"

"Let's see. I'm guessing six or seven."

"Mr. Stern, I'm not buying it."

"What Lieutenant, what do you see?"

"He's got another supplier."

"How do you get that?"

"Let me look at these things from his phone."

Angelina stood up and laid out the piles of transcripts. "Lt. Mehle, these are the transcripts from Avery's phone. The sticky notes are on the pages we got questionable phone numbers. The red highlighter is from the phone numbers we thought were possible drug numbers. The blue highlighters are from the one we think may be his girlfriend.”

“Got it, Ms.”

“Call me Angelina.

“Ok, Angelina it is.” He began to pore over the piles of transcripts. “Who has seen these?”

“Lou Dawson has a copy of the transcripts, but he hasn’t done the work we did. We did ask him about one number. It seems this one here, (I pointed to four red highlighted ones) belongs to Meg Keely’s cell phone, Lt. Keely’s six year old daughter.”

“Oh, not good. Let me see. 17 calls in four months to this phone.”

“How many numbers have at least four calls in four months?”

“We can get that for you.”

“No, that’s Ok, I have to do this in-house.”

“Does anyone else recognize some of these numbers so we can cut down on our work?”

“He has a woman he lives with, or lived with. She probably could recognize some of these numbers.”

“The more we eliminate from our search, the faster we narrow down our investigation.” “I’ll call her in. She didn’t want to come in before because she thought it might reveal where Avery was, and she didn’t want to help him get caught.”

“That’s not why I want her.”

“Of course, I’ll tell her that.”

I got Alison on the phone at work. “Alison”.

“Is this you Peter? It’s Aliyah.”

“Ok, Aliyah. I’ve got a police lieutenant here and he is tracing a number of phone calls on Andy’s phone. We’ve got tons and it could take hours to go through. We thought you could help by eliminating some of those you recognize.”

“I told you no before.”

“True. But, remember Andy lost the whole benefit of his

plea deal by skipping out on his bail."

"Peter, he's never coming back, he won't go to jail, not ever. So I won't help get him a deal again."

"Ok, but at least you'll know where he is now." "By looking up his prior contacts?"

"Exactly."

"Ok, I'll look, but I won't help."

"Fair enough."

"When do you want me?"

"After work today. You're just around the corner."

"Ok, I'll be there at 5:00."

"See you then."

We left Lt. Mehle and his assistant in the conference room to go over the call transcript in more detail. After an hour, he came back.

"Peter, I think we've made out some of the patterns here."

"What you got?"

"If I am deciphering the drug talk properly, not only were they selling him a quarter ki of coke at $5,000, but they were acting as guards for him. They walked him into the rave on Friday afternoon and walked him to his car on Friday and Saturday nights at 2:00 a.m. The coke they were selling him was already bagged with another gang's stamp on it."

"What other gang?"

"A lot of different extra gangs. So, there's an obvious answer here. Those bags were from previous arrests of other dealers. The cops were holding back bags from their arrests and giving it to Avery to sell."

"So, it was cops, not another gang." "That might be true."

Alison came in at 5:00 as promised. Angelina and Carmen stayed late to watch over her review of the phone records. They were not going to miss the melodrama when she found the other girlfriend. Alison sat at the conference room table while Angelina explained the piles and the highlighter in blue and red. I was at my desk catching up on a few late phone calls.

Then I heard a shriek. Some of those leaving the office late were crowding at the small conference room door. I brushed past and saw Alison with a stack of pages in her hand. "That bastard, that low life, that fucking . . ." She was obviously now aware of Avery's other girl friend. Poor Alison probably didn't deserve all this. Her mammoth temper tantrum in front of about 15 people from my office. I put my arm around her and pulled the conference room door shut. She was crying and sniffling in my arms.

"That bastard. He was living with me, I paid the rent, he had my car and he was running up to Drexel for his little college girl." Then she saw the printout from Facebook Angelina had put on the table. "Blond bitch." A new strain of obscenities. "I'll get him. I'll get that fucker.

I'll cut his balls off and stuff them in his mouth." It certainly was a credible threat. She was a passionate woman. She slowly calmed down.

I had to ask. "Aliyah, do you want me to find him now?" I wasn't proud of myself. I had manipulated her into betraying her boyfriend. Although I have to admit I got some pleasure at further revealing to her what a shit he was.

"Yes, get the bastard."

"Can you review his phone records and, maybe, figure out where he went? You said he had friends down south."

"Oh, I know them. I can recognize their number. They're in South Carolina, near Savannah. Angelina was on it in a second.

"Peter, that's area code 912." She and Carmen started flipping through the pages.

"No, wait. They live in a little town on the side of a river. If you say the name of the town, I'll remember."

So, Angelina pulled up a Google map around Savannah and started to list the towns on rivers. This wasn't producing much. We couldn't find anything on the transcripts with a 912 area code.

"Maybe, it's in an area code outside 912." Then, a light bulb went on inside Alison's head. "Wait, wait Peter. This may be something. You know where he did those raves. Well, people kind of live there and wall off a bedroom for themselves in the building. I think he kept a little hideaway there. I'll bet if we follow this blond bitch there, we'll find Avery.

"Ok, that's an idea. I'll call Dawson. We'll try to tail this Czpanski girl."

I got on the phone with Dawson and Mehle. They agreed to put some surveillance on this girl for a few days. Alison still kept snarling and posing with clenched fists. "Hell hath no fury." Angelina brought her a can of Sprite which she sipped and sat back in the chair.

"Are you happy now, Peter, seeing me like this?" She said this in front of just my crew fortunately.

"Aliyah, I take no pleasure in this. But you'll be fine. You have guts. You'll survive."

"Yeah, but maybe I'll get even." She calmed down finally and left.

It didn't take long for Mehle and his minions to track down Cheryl Czpanski, but she did not seem interested in going to the rave building. She lived in the dorm at Drexel.

So Mehle proposed that we do a raid on the rave buildings on Lancaster Avenue at about 6:30 a.m. Always a good time to get people unaware. He notified the building, electric and plumbing inspectors for the City's Department of License and Inspections. For some reason, these buildings along Lancaster

Avenue had managed to survive despite many obvious violations. The presence of the City's inspectors gave the raid some legitimacy.

They hit the rave building itself first. The inspectors were busy snapping pictures and writing up violations as Mehle and two others walked down the hallways.

"Whoa! Lieutenant, something here." As they pushed aside the plywood makeshift door, a man lay flat on his back, inert with a small pool of blood at the back of his head. Mehle ran up and inspected the body and pulled up an image on his phone. Yes, it was Avery Witherspoon, not long dead.

Soon, a phalanx of forensic people, a gaggle from the coroner's office, a fleet from homicide descended on the building and mounted the elderly wooden stairs to where Avery lay.

Mehle stood outside in the hallway with the Coroner and a homicide detective. "So what do we have, Mack?"

Horace Horan, the Coroner was an older paunchy fellow, who peered up over his glasses. "Two small gunshot wounds to the medulla oblongata – rear of the skull. Dead a few hours. Total rigor, liver mortis, complete. The blood has settled to the lowest point in the body so at least 12 hours. I'd say yesterday afternoon. Bullet entry wounds consistent with small caliber."

"Not a police weapon?" Mehle had his suspicions.

"No, maybe a .32 or .22. Close range. I'll probably get gun powder residue. Shot within three feet looks like."

"Any struggle, defensive wounds?"

"Not that I can see."

"Thanks, Mack." He went back to the body, now on a stretcher to be carried downstairs to the morgue's van.

The homicide detective, an older veteran, Harvey Vongole, in a rumpled suit (somehow the detective bureau issues these older rumpled suits to the detectives once they get their promotions) asked Mehle, "So Lieutenant what are you doing here and who is good for this?"

"Harvey, come on up to IA headquarters and I'll let you review my file."

"Are cops involved?"

"Maybe." Mehle and Vongole walked down the stairs shaking their heads.

I was asked to join the meeting with Lt. Mehle and Detective MacPherson out at IA headquarters. After a consultation with the police commissioner, it was agreed that the murder investigation would be headed up by Lt. Mehle and assisted by MacPherson. Lou Dawson was asked to attend as well. I arrived about 2:00 p.m. and was ushered into a drab warren of metal desks to a back room office. I had brought my file with me.

I was asked first to brief the two about everything from Avery's shooting on Apple Street to the present. Mehle and Dawson had already heard most of what I had to say, but this was all new to MacPherson. A patrolman came in to copy most of my file as I laid it out in order of my presentation. MacPherson took a few notes and asked a few questions.

"So, Mr. Stern, who do you think did it?"

"My client was murdered, I was released from most of my confidential duties, but since he never had cooperated with me anyway, there wasn't much I had to conceal. They were interested now in the box of evidence I had received from the Phantoms."

"So they just gave it to you and wanted Witherspoon to cooperate?"

"That's about it. I don't think Witherspoon knew what was included, but he okayed me turning it over for a plea deal."

"Would the Phantoms want to kill him?"

"I can't think why; except that they wanted to take over the DJ slot at the rave. It was very profitable."

"But this Witherspoon was going to jail for at least five years, even with a plea deal. So they would get the spot anyway."

"True."

"So, the Dogs, revenge maybe?"

"Could be. My information never came from Witherspoon, but they didn't know that. On the other hand, he did have a shootout with them on Apple Street, which blew up their whole operation."

"Could be."

Mehle rumbled, "I see the narco cops who supplied Witherspoon with confiscated bags from their arrests. They kept guard for him when he brought in the drugs and took out the cash. He could rat them out. I like them for it."

Dawson broke in. "Look, this was a low caliber pistol he was shot in the back of the head, there was no struggle. It could have been this ex-girl friend. She was pretty mad."

MacPherson said, "It could be lots of people. We need more work on this." "I think the cops did this, so I'll handle that angle," Lt. Mehle volunteered.

"I'll take the ex-girlfriend," MacPherson offered. I winced at that. Could they really suspect her?

I had to ask. "One thing we don't know is how they knew to find Avery in the rave building. Someone knew he kept this place."

"Good point." Did Alison know where it was?

It didn't take long for Mehle and MacPherson to bring in a number of cops to interview the buildings residents. This proved to be a difficult task since the residents were often anti-government, anti-social and never liked cops. They claimed, probably true, that Avery/Andy was known as the DJ, didn't spend much time in the building and was not very sociable with them. It seemed none had heard any shots.'

Mehle brought in Cheryl Czpanski to the detective district headquarters. She was not as enticing as her Facebook picture. She was a tall, awkward girl of 19. She had tattoos on both arms and a piercing on her lip. Her hair hung straight in a dull blond. She had been whisked off the Drexel campus and was very frightened and teary in the small office.

"Am I guilty of something?"

"No . . . no." Mehle assured her in a calm voice. She seemed to calm down. "This is about Andy, the DJ. Do you know him?"

She looked down. Reluctantly she admitted, "We dated some."

Mehle knew better than to broach the drug issue as yet, or even Andy's death. "Had you been to the raves?"

"Yes."

"Did you know Andy kept a place in the rave building?" "Yes," she ventured shyly.

"Did you ever meet him there?" A shy yes.

"Were you angry with him?"

"Not really. He did hit on other girls, but that was about it." "Did you use coke or meth together?"

"Oh, I don't know."

"We're not interested in drug possession."

"Well, he would have a few people to his place at the rave and we'd get high."

"So, Cheryl, I have to tell you that Andy is dead." She looked like she'd been hit with a hammer, her head flung back.

"What . . . who . . ." "Did you know this?"

"No . . . no." She started to cry. "Were you close?"

"No . . . not really. Just a fun person to hang out with." "Do you know anyone who was angry with him."

"He told me about his ex who lived in Fishtown and was an older woman. I don't know if they broke up, but he said she was jealous and he was through with her.

"Did you know her name?" "No . . . just an older woman."

"Did you see him selling drugs?"

"If he's dead, I guess I can say 'yes'."

"Did he have anyone helping him, like keeping watch, or protecting him?" "Maybe, I couldn't say. He had guys hang around. I didn't know them." "Could you identify them if you saw their pictures?"

"Maybe not. But they had short haircuts and were white." Mehle looked at MacPherson, raised his eyebrows. MacPherson shrugged. "Ok, Cheryl, we'll take you back to the campus. You've been helpful. Please don't tell anyone about this investigation."

She still looked like a frightened deer, but she pushed her chair back and followed MacPherson to his unmarked car.

I wasn't in the office more than two minutes when I got a call from Alison. "Peter, why are you so late coming into work?" It was 9:15 a.m.

"Is this Alison? I might be late when I just have paperwork. What do you want?"

"It's Aliyah. I'm here at some police station. They want to question me."

"What about?" I already knew of Avery's death by now and guessed they would want to question her.

"Andy's murder. Did you know about it? Why didn't you tell me. What do they want?

Can you get here?"

"Calm down. First, did they read you your rights?" "No. Should they?"

"At this point you are not a suspect. So you can relax, they just want information." "Suspect? Do they think I murdered Andy?"

"I didn't say that. They will want to know where you were about the time of his death." "So I am a suspect."

"No, they have to rule you out. Where are you?"

"55th and Pine." I had represented her for free before concerning the forfeiture of her car. She now was presuming to have me represent her for free once again. It triggered in my mind that she was my ex-girlfriend who deserted me while I was in the military. I was a corporate lawyer type, my hourly rate was pretty high. She would never pay it, and would freak out if I asked her to. But I figured maybe two or three hours calming her down as the police asked her a few questions. So I kept things calm. I took an Uber up to 55th and Pine. I could hear her yelling at the detective as I walked in. He looked relieved to see me. Rarely had I been greeted so warmly by the cops. Mehle and MacPherson sat at a table facing Alison. They got up. "Counselor, can you calm her down. We need to ask her some questions about Witherspoon's homicide."

"Yes Lieutenant, happy to help." They left.

"Now, look Alison, you shut up and calm down. If you don't, they can book you for the murder." She started to take a deep breath to launch into a tirade. "You are a spoiled woman. You get no special treatment here. They can ask you what they want and you will cooperate or else."

"But Peter, Andy's dead. . . . and it's Aliyah . . ."

"Yes, I know and you're upset. And, by the way, it's not Aliyah. I saw your driver's license and the police verified your name."

"Ok, ok. What do I do?" I gave her the advice that all lawyers give their clients. Listen to the question, answer the question unless I tell you not to. Answer only the question that's asked. Don't put in a whole lot of unnecessary details. Details are what get you in trouble. Of course, few clients listened to this advice and go on blabbing anyway. I waved the men back in.

Mehle started in a calm even tone. "Did you know Avery Witherspoon?"

"Yes. We lived together for three years before he left." Ah, more details.

"So why did he leave?"

"I think he was afraid of going to prison."

"Did he sell drugs?"

"I would assume so."

"Did you use drugs?"

"No. I resent that."

I waved to calm her down. She looked at me indignantly. "When was the last time you saw him?" She stared at the ceiling.

"OK, he left Tuesday night, but left his things here. He came back Wednesday when I was at work and took his stuff in some van. I didn't see him after that."

"What are your work hours?"

"9 to 5". She sang the Dolly Parton song.

"Do you work late ever?"

"Not usually."

"Can you verify your work hours? Do you clock in?"

"I'm not some factory worker. "Oh, wait . . . I think the building has a closed circuit camera in the lobby and there is a sign in/out sheet at the lobby desk."

'So what did you do after work on Tuesday and Wednesday?" She looked at me, apparently angry now.

"Nothing. I live alone (another glare at me). I made dinner and watched TV."

"Did anyone see you during that time?"

"Not that I know of." "Do you own a gun?"

"No. What do I need a gun for? . . . Oh, yes. No, I don't own a gun."

"Did you know Mr. Witherspoon kept a place at a building on Lancaster Avenue?"

"Yeah, he kept a place to store his stuff . . ." Oh no, I could feel the heat . . . keep quiet . . . oh no! "And to fuck his little coed bitches while they smoked weed." Oh no!

"So you knew about his recent girlfriend?"

"Yes, Mr. Stern here was kind enough to show me the phone calls on his cell and her Facebook page, the little tramp."

"Were you angry about that?"

"Fuck yeah!" Then she looked over at me. I sighed and held my head.

"Would you have been angry enough to kill him?"

A big pause . . . a sigh, . . very dramatic. "I suppose I was through with him. No. I wasn't mad that he had been screwing some dingbat coed. I was mad that I had been played for a fool." Ok, good answer.

Mehle and MacPherson got up to confer to see if any more questions were needed.

"Oh, Peter. I've been such a dope. Can you forgive me?" She started to cry. I patted her on the back. "I'm ashamed in front of you."

"Don't worry about that."

The detectives came back in and let Alison go for the time being.

We shared an Uber back to Center City. As all clients – even non-paying ones ask – "Did I do alright?" We never get them upset so we just say they were fine, even though they blabbered too much. As it was, I thought Alison had been too angry at Avery. It was not just a breakup, but it was a bold in-your-face betrayal. Could she have killed him? Maybe. The shots were to the back of the head with no struggle, by a small caliber pistol – a lady's weapon. It was possible, but I liked the dirty cops who had been supplying Avery. They needed a cover up and from a man who it appeared who had already cooperated to get a lighter sentence. Yes, I liked them better for it. The small caliber gun would have been a nice distraction.

"So, Alison, did you ever know that Avery was being supplied his drugs by cops?"

"Avery did say he had cops who were his friends. He implied he was paying them off."

"Did you ever know he was making a lot of money from these drug sales? Not just what you found."

"No."

"Now I believe he was buying large quantities on his own and making a lot more."

"That bastard. He never told me and he never helped out with the rent. He got what he deserved, the low life."

We were quiet the rest of the way and parted ways after City Hall. I hoped this was the end of it.

Once again, I went to my favorite sandwich place and was seated in my usual booth. As I walked in, my favorite waitress, Helen, ordered a tuna fish on white toast and an iced tea as I read a Daily News someone had left on one of the tables.

A man came up and slipped into the seat across from me. He was the same guy who was from the Phantoms before who had asked me to cooperate on Avery's behalf and would give me a box of evidence against the Dogs. He was a slim Hispanic guy with a Dodgers baseball cap. Why do all the Latinos wear Dodgers caps? I mean the Phillies had plenty of Latinos and we sent them Utley and Rollins.

"Hello, Mr. Stern. Do you remember me?"

"Certainly." I was beginning to suspect he would want his $35,000 back since Avery was now dead.

"What can I do for you?"

'I have more information to give you."

"Ah, I see."

"Now that Avery is dead and will not be cooperating further with the police . . ."

"Oh, you want your money back?"

"No, . . . no. But I have something of interest to your friend Lt. Mehle."

"About Avery's murder?"

"Not quite."

"Why me?"

"You were dependable before and you got a lot of our money."

"True."

"So, what is this new evidence?"

"Lots of stuff against the dirty narc cops. Lt. Mehle is interested in them. And he and this Detective MacPherson like them for the murder of your boy Avery."

"How do you know that?" I got a shrug. "So you want to see these cops convicted?"

"Yes. It eliminates competitors. Not only does it get them out of West Philly, but it will invalidate their ability to testify against drug dealers. Once they are found dirty, they will never get past cross-examination."

"Uh-huh."

"How about the murder?"

"Can't say anything about that."

"Did the cops do it to silence him?"

"Can't say."

"Can't or won't."

"Look, Mr. Stern, the box will be delivered to your office. You can keep the $35,000. You cooperated like we said. You can deliver the evidence to Lt. Mehle or not, whatever you want." He slid out of my booth and was gone.

I saw these revolving issues in my mind. I no longer had a client, he was dead. I had received two separate payments, one to have him refuse to cooperate, one to have him cooperate. I asked for neither and made no deal either way. He had never in fact cooperated, I had. He never made a guilty plea in court. The Dogs were nearly out of business now due to the Phantoms' information against them. So I could keep the money and do nothing.

Now, Avery was dead. Alison was a possible but remote suspect. The cops who supplied him with confiscated drugs were most likely the culprits. And now, I would hold in my hands evidence against them probably as good as the stuff I had gotten earlier from the Phantoms against the Dogs. It would implicate dirty narco cops. It would definitely aid Lt. Mehle and rid the streets of some drugs and dealers, but it would advance the cause of the Phantoms – soon to be a large and powerful criminal enterprise in West Philly. What to do? I knew the answer.

Run it by Digby. If I explained my dilemmas out loud to him, I often answered my own question.

I phoned Digby's office on my way in and got Betty James, his secretary, paralegal and general watchdog for many years. "Yo, Betty, is Digby in? I got a few questions."

"Peter, why is it you always ask Digby the most questions?"

"Betty, I sail a very fine tack against the wind."

"I'll bet you do. He has a 1:30 that will be short. Just an elderly lady changing her Will."

"Those blue hairs love Digby."

"Now, now Peter, it pays lots of bills."

"I'll be around about 2:00."

"See you then."

At 2:00 I was just coming around as Digby was saying

goodbye to Muffy. He waved me into his office as he walked Muffy to our lobby.

"So, Peter, what's going on?" I knew Digby always liked my narratives. In his day, he had done it all – criminal law, divorces, angry lawsuits. Now, he was clipping the coupons on a lifetime's work building a reputation and a law practice. Mostly older women who survived their spouses and had no idea what to do with their money.

I rebriefed Digby on Avery's shootout on Apple Street, the $35,000 from the Phantoms, my delivery of the Phantom's box of evidence, etc. up until Avery's death and my conference with Lt. Mehle and the homicide detective.

"So, who does Mehle suspect?"

"Probably dirty narco cops, but a lingering doubt as to Alison."

"Your old girlfriend?"

"Yeah, her."

"You don't represent her?"

"No."

"That's good. Once you have sex with a female client, they never want to pay you."

"That was long ago, Digby."

"True, but were you paid when you rescued her car from confiscation?"

"Well, no."

"See what I mean. Your white knight instincts take over and they revert to being pre-lib when it comes to money."

"Harsh, Digby, harsh."

"Ah, but true."

"Not you Digby?" I couldn't hide my smirk.

"Alas, I do not kiss and tell. So anyway, the cops like dirty narco cops."

"True so far. Now, I'm at lunch and the same guy from the Phantoms slides into my booth. He wants to have me deliver another box of evidence, this time to Mehle and this time, against the cops. I haven't got the box yet, but he promises it has good stuff, just as before. Now, I don't represent anybody. We have $70,000 in cash in the office safe."

"And you want to know what to do with the money and the box."

"Yes."

First, the $35,000 that the Dogs gave you was under the condition that you not have Avery cooperate, but you did on his behalf. Under pure contract law, we do not have the right to retain this money, but we do not wish to return money gotten from drug sales to the drug dealers. In addition, they no longer exist because the box of evidence you turned over on Avery's behalf has resulted in the Dogs gang being rolled up by law enforcement. So we retain the money for a reasonable period of time to see if there are any legitimate claimants and then, there being none, we donate this to charity.

"Second, the other $35,000 was on the condition that Avery cooperate, which you did on his behalf. That money was legitimately earned. Since the cooperation resulted in the arrest of many members of a drug gang, we have contributed to the public good. Nice work Peter. Now, this new box of evidence was delivered without fee or conditions. We do not represent a client here and are ordinary private citizens. If we turn this box over, we expose a new bunch of corrupt police officers, but also benefit incidentally a drug gang by ridding them of a number of competitors. Since the legal system relies on the integrity of our police officers, this is a higher principle to be pursued rather than the possible future financial benefit to a drug gang. So, we turn the box over to Lt. Mehle.

"Are the drug gang the possible suspects in Avery's murder, in order to frame the corrupt police and provoke an investigation?" I would say that this can be a strong possibility. It is unlikely that Avery would alter his past behavior and inform on his drug suppliers, and his murder could draw attention to the arrangement the corrupt police had with Avery. It is a possibility worthy of further investigation.

"Ah, Digby. Well done. I have to agree."

"Since we now have no living client, I suggest we refrain from getting further involved in this matter since it may draw us into a tar baby. For your own good, I would avoid representing Alison. Dispose of the box of evidence to Lt. Mehle and avoid further entanglements."

"I can see that. We certainly do not need my name or the firm's appearing in the media."

"Quite so." I thanked Digby for his help and returned to my office.

Sure enough, neatly copied pages of transcripts of conversations, photographs and CD's were delivered to my office. None of the conversations came from illegally tapped telephone calls, but from highly sensitive parabolic microphones. Conversations in open air are fair game and those mikes pick up everything. Someone was capable of sophisticated investigations. I re- wrapped the box, after copying everything, just in case, and had it hand delivered to Lt. Mehle.

I considered poor Avery Witherspoon's case over.   I thankfully sat in the conference room with Angelina, organized the files and put them into storage boxes to be stored in the vault for the next office cleaning. Frankly, I was finished with Avery and I might add Alison/Aliyah.

While I still had some pieces of shrapnel lodged in my brain from our long ago relationship, the past few months had given me some closure. Although not what I really had sought for the long haul, I now had business problems and rich people's problems to worry about. And it was always peaceful when I could go back to the library and spend some hours researching my way through the law books. I was sitting in front of four big books trying to follow some judge's reasoning when my cell rang.

"Peter, it's for you. Lt. Mehle, you want him?" Angelina was my gatekeeper.

"Ok, might as well."

"Mr. Stern,"

"Yes, Lieutenant, what's up? Do we have Avery's murderer?"

"No. So far these crooked cops are tight as ticks. They have free lawyers and clam up. They know what jail means for a convicted cop."

"How about the crooked ones from the Phantom's box?"

"Oh, that was a big help. Lots of resignations, lots of guilty pleas so long as we send them to Cremona." He was talking about the old man's prison past Reading. They kept prisoners who needed medical attention and was usually easy time. The cops turned out to be good health aides and they were an hour's drive from Philadelphia.

"So, what can I do for you?"

"We have a big box of Avery's belongings we took out of Alison's apartment. We're through sifting among them for evidence. You were his attorney, so I want to send them to you."

"Oh no, Lieutenant. I'm done with those people."

"Well, there's his mother and father who are separated and not talking. There's his two girlfriends. So we need someone to sort through who gets what."

I could feel myself drawn back in, like an old scab getting pulled off. Very reluctantly and only because Lt. Mehle asked, I agreed.

The next day a UPS box was sitting outside the office as I returned from lunch.

Avery's Heirs

I had hoped this was over, but now I had to perform one of those rituals that Wills and Estates lawyers perform. Angelina had notified all of Avery's nearest heirs to our office to divide up the personal effects. Lt. Mehle had sent a box by UPS and Angelina had created a list of the items. They consisted of whatever was in Alison's apartment, the rave storage space and hideaway, the van, and on Avery's person. They were to be laid out on a conference room table and picked over by the heirs with whom we had to make small talk. Usually if the family had money, the estates lawyers would buttonhole the heirs and get them to prepare their Wills with us. Since Avery had nothing, was a ne'er do well, and was mostly a pain in the ass, the prospect of the gathering was dismal. His legal heirs were his mother and father, long separated and not enthusiastic about being in the same room together. To complicate matters, Alison checked in and insisted that she attend the session. Apparently, Lt. Mehle had called her to see if she wished to retrieve items which were hers. I certainly sensed no love lost on Avery from her at this point. Her insistence on attending this little ceremony was not welcome. But she was invited.

Our guests trundled in and, thankfully, were greeted by Angelina while I hung back in my office. When I was buzzed by Angelina, I came down the hall and was met by Alison

"Peter, can I choose something?"

"I'm sorry, Alison but you are not an intestate heir. He left no Will or any children, so only his parents are next in line. Maybe they'll let you take something of sentimental value if you ask nicely. It's up to them. Nothing here has any value."

I saw her go back in and sit with Avery's parents while I checked the list.   It was a motley collection of odd bits and pieces. After everyone had browsed through everything with little comment, Alison grabbed my elbow and asked me again to step outside.

"Peter, I would like to have that picture, the framed watercolor of some water birds, that's mine. Avery took it when he left."

About this time, Lt. Mehle came in quietly and sat in the corner of the conference room. The Witherspoons, both of whom had been asked a few questions for the murder investigation, eyed him warily.

"Ok, Alison, I'll ask."

"Peter, it's Aliyah."

"Oh, that again. Ok, Aliyah, I'll ask." I turned to the Witherspoons in the conference room.. "Is there anything in particular you want? If it has any real value, I can get it appraised, but it seems like mostly . . . er . . . keepsakes to me."

The Witherspoons shrugged. Mr. Witherspoon was not close to his son and had no sentimental attachment to anything. Nor did Avery's mother. She was still shaken by Avery's death and the discovery that he had been a drug dealer, so she was weeping quietly, but managed a few glares at her husband.

"Mr. and Mrs. Witherspoon, you are each the legal heirs of Avery and entitled to one half of his estate, since he left no Will saying otherwise. Ms. Rosen here wishes to ask for that watercolor if you have no objections." Ms. Witherspoon waved her hand dismissively and Mr. Witherspoon examined it briefly and shrugged his shoulders.

Alison/Aliyah thanked them both and picked up the picture

frame; it was about 12 inches by 15 inches.

If no one wants anything, I will deliver it to Goodwill down the street." "Fine by me," the Witherspoons echoed.

"In that case, we are done." Angelina started to put the items back into the UPS box as I walked the Witherspoons to the door.

"Mr. Stern." Uh oh, when Lt. Mehle called me that I knew I would have a problem. "I have to ask you to join me for this afternoon."

I wasn't going for the bait. "What's up, Lieutenant, I thought I was done."

"You're gonna want to see this." Carmen had been hovering around the conference room and my office, whispering with Angelina.

"Peter, can I come too?" Carmen wanted in on any action.

"Are you working on anything important?" I didn't have to ask this question. Carmen could smell an adventure. Whatever she was working on would not be important, even if it were the Versailles Treaty.

"No."

"Ok, come along then."

"Missy," Lt. Mehle broke in. "I may need you to change. Can you look like a boy?" Carmen was petite, when not dressed to look like a sex pot, she could. It did not take her long to change into jeans, a sweatshirt, a baseball cap and sneakers. She was ready and passed muster.

We went down to Lt. Mehle's car and drove out to a health club in the Northeast. Mehle and I each brought along workout bags. We parked in the large parking lot. Lt. Mehle went in and checked out the place. He returned to sit in his unmarked car with us.

"What are we waiting for?" I had to ask.

"You'll see."

We sent Carmen out for snacks and drinks and sat. This was one of the jobs in police work I never liked. A long boring stakeout.

Carmen had her earphones in and Latin rhythms poured out as Mehle and I listened to the news station.

It was unmistakable then, a red Audi A3 pulled in and parked near the health club. A slim figure in jeans, a leather jacket and a baseball cap got out and went into the club.

"Here we go." Lt. Mehle bounced out of the driver's side and we hurried to keep up.

Mehle flashed his badge as we went to the front desk and then on into the men's locker room. "It's number 316." Mehle mumbled as we went to the edge of the row of lockers. There

midway in the row stood the thin figure in jeans and leather jacket putting a key in the lock. When she had pulled out a large gym bag and was resting on the bench, Mehle moved in.

" Ms. Alison Rosen, put your hands up."

"The face under the brim of the baseball cap jerked up. Yes, it was Alison, with her hair up under a baseball cap. She was holding the gym bag and a key.

"Wha . . . what's this about?" By that time, two uniformed officers appeared out of nowhere. Mehle turned to them.

"Cuff her." He started to read Miranda warnings to her. Alison started to cry when she saw me at the end of the row.

"Peter, I can't bear you to see me like this." One of the officers was female and started to pat Alison down and take her key.

"Ms. Rosen, you are charged with the murder of Avery Witherspoon."

"No . . . no . . . Peter do something." The other officer took the gym bag and pulled out a roll of bright yellow tape and wrapped it up over the zipper.

Mehle turned to me. "It was the painting she took. We found the key inside the paper on the back. We traced the key with a logo to this club.:

"So she figured out what the key did?"

"She must have known the picture disappeared when he moved out. It had been there when we searched the apartment the first time. I guess she either got him to tell where the painting was, or she found it. Either way, she had to kill him so she could have sole possession of the money."

"So, Lieutenant, you lured her into taking the picture."

"Yes, we already knew the key was there and it belonged to the locker. There's about $300,000 in that gym bag."

I never suspected Alison of this, but she was an intense woman. She found out how much he was making from drugs and not sharing with her. I'm sure the capper was the Drexel co-ed on the side.

As she was being lead away, she kept saying, "Peter do something." I just could thank my lucky stars this woman was not in my life.

Discussion re: Alison's Arrest

When our daughter had left the dining table that night, either to do her homework or play social media on her phone, I told my wife about Alison's arrest at the health club. Her reaction annoyed me. After staring into space for a few minutes she said, "Peter, you have to help her."

I didn't know where this was coming from. Wives are usually expected to be jealous or wary of former girlfriends. Maybe, this is an unfair stereotype. Maybe she felt a kinship with Alison by her connection to me. Something told me I would not understand this reaction, so I just asked why. Now Lynn had not been educated in law or in forensic investigation, but she did have common sense, which is all we ever ask of our juries. But I had sometimes run the facts of some of my cases past her to see what her reaction might be. Of course, I was always careful not to get into confidential information. I certainly did not want anyone to try to pump her for the inside dope on a case, or worse yet, threaten her to have her reveal something dangerous. Now this was strange. Alison had not been my client, except when I had to retrieve her car from being confiscated. I never went into any details about Avery and all his shenanigans, but it seemed Lynn had seen something I hadn't.

"Well, Peter, just because she found his money doesn't mean she killed him."

I explained that the gun that killed Avery was a small caliber .22 or .32. These are usually considered to be women's weapons of choice since they don't have much of a kick. "So, that's a good distraction. A good way to frame her."

"Ok, but there was no struggle. Avery was shot execution style in the back of the head.

So he knew his assailant."

"True, but could be anyone holding a gun on him, getting him to behave and turn around."

"I can see that. Ok.   Maybe she knew about the key to the locker at the health club.

Maybe she wanted him dead so he wouldn't find out she would use it and take the money.

"Yes. She obviously wanted the money. She's in trouble on that score, but he had already left her and was looking at a long prison sentence if he ever came back. So, why should she kill him? Why not just get him arrested? He'd be as good as dead."

"Hmm. Ok so far. But, look I am tired of this whole matter. I'm still angry and disgusted with Alison. I don't want to get back into it. And I have too many emotions about this whole thing. Her lawyer should be objective, able to look at the case from a distance."

"Oh, poo! She needs your help. You're a good lawyer. She doesn't need some hack.

She knows you'll do your best for her."

"Oh no, Lynn. I want to put this all behind me."

"But you know the whole story. What if these crooked narcotics cops did him in to keep him from ratting them out?"

"Yes, but she has no credibility against all those cops."

"Now, no regular criminal defense attorney is going to want to go after the police and continue to practice in this city. You're not regular.   You don't have much of a criminal practice. If you go after them, they can't touch you and it won't affect your practice."

"Whoa, Lynn. You're making a good case. Let me think about this." "Good boy, Peter. Try to do the right thing."

"So, you don't think you'd be jealous."

Lynn laughed. "Peter, we've been married ten years now. I know you. You like having a family, a house, a position in a law firm. You're respected. You like all that. Besides, you couldn't put up with a nut case like that for more than ten seconds, she'd drive you crazy."

"Well, that's true."

"So, think about it."

Dr. Rosen

I didn't get much time to think. The next morning as I was catching up on the details of my cases, the receptionist buzzed me. "Dr. Rosen is here to see you."

Oh no, Dr. Rosen was a very decent guy. He had been very disappointed that Alison had dumped me back then. He wanted me for a son-in-law. Now he was here to talk to me about Alison's arrest. I still didn't want to do it, but I couldn't seem to get my hand out of this tar baby. It just kept pulling me back.

Angelina brought Dr. Rosen back and gave me the Italian eye roll as she turned back to her desk. She never liked Alison and wanted out of this mess as much as I did. She didn't like Alison and didn't want me to represent her.

"Peter, good to see you again."

"Thanks, Doc. Well, not the best of circumstances."

"So, let me get to the point. I know you're busy. Can you get Alison out of this? I don't know much about the law, but I know Alison wouldn't shoot anyone."

"Well, Doc, I'm probably a little too close to this whole thing. I don't know if I could be objective."

"Now, I know you're a good lawyer and you already know the whole case. Besides, Alison and I trust you."

"It's a very difficult case. I may have to investigate some bad narcotics cops and they are not only very street smart but dangerous."

"It's just that I know I can rely on you to do the best job. You may still be mad at Alison, even after all these years, but I know you can be professional."

"Let me think about this, will you?"

"Sure, sure." I hated to say no to Dr. Rosen. He was a genuinely decent person and deserved my full attention. Between him and Lynn, I was feeling a mountain of guilt. I knew who to talk to, however: Digby.

Later that day, Ms. James, Digby's personal assistant, stopped by my office. "Peter, Digby can see you now." So, up to the corner office I went.

Digby Consult re: Alison

I reluctantly walked down the hall to the corner office and found Digby leaning back in his chair and staring out at the Philadelphia port. As I came in, Digby without turning said, "So, you want to know if you should represent Ms. Rosen in her murder trial?"

"Yes. How did you figure this out?"

"Pete, you were in too deep. You know all the facts and she will need you. Peter, you are such a boy scout, you will not be able to resist aiding a damsel in distress."

"Ok, so what do I do?"

"You get her out on bail and have her and her father come see me about fee arrangements. I don't want the firm to become a charitable institution, and you will sell-out cheap because you will be maneuvered into feeling guilty."

I nodded. He turned around to face me. "Now, several cautions. First don't fuck female clients or you'll never get paid."

"No, no. Those days are over."

"Yeah, sure. The libido always trumps the pocketbook." "No, I've learned my lesson with her."

"Ok, good so far. So I don't need to put a clothespin on your member."

"I hear you. Yes. No clothespin."

"This thing with accusing dirty cops, work closely with Internal Affairs and document everything. You could easily be caught in the middle of some very bad politics. If you get anything on them, it will blow up and be an investigation for years to come. Document everything and bring along that little Latina when you talk to someone. Have her record everything."

"Yes. Carmen. She'll be there."

"Of course, pull all the cops' personnel files."

"Angelina is already typing up the subpoena. But Digby, you still haven't answered my first question."

"Should you do it? Of course, you can't avoid it and you already know you can win it. Am I right?"

"Ok." I could see years of pain ahead of me. This tar baby had got its hold on me. As I got back to the office, I saw a neat stack of subpoenas Angelina had already typed up. It was inevitable. I was in.

I went to the bail hearing with Dr. Rosen, which would be a very perfunctory matter. The judge quickly set a bond of $100,000. That meant a cash deposit of $10,000. Her father had come to the hearing with four $5,000 cashier's checks in case the bail was higher. I walked him down to the cashier's window.

"So, Doc, our senior partner wants to see you and Alison about fee arrangements. Is that ok?"

"Yes Peter. Thank you. I didn't want to talk money with you."

We walked over to the holding cells and retrieved Alison, looking tired, weepy and bedraggled.

Her father asked, "Alison, do you want to go see Peter's senior partner now or do you want to rest first?"

"Rest, Pop. I'm worn out. And you, Peter. Are you going to help me?"

"It looks that way. If you want somebody else, that's your right."

"Screw that. I want you. Is that alright?" She turned to her father.

"Sure, dear. When you're ready we'll talk fee arrangements with Peter's boss."

"What, no family discounts?"

 "Alison please, I want to be business-like about this."

"Don't worry, Dr. Rosen, Digby will give you a break."

Dr. Rosen and Alison went to their parking lot and I took the subway back to the office. I was putting together a list in my head of what I had to do.

Analysis of Alison's Case

Now that I was inextricably in this mess, my mind began to focus on the way to proceed. If not Alison, who would kill Avery? With what I knew about his hidden side deal with the cops, they were my first and, now I guess, only option. But narco cops are a tight knit bunch and a very street smart wary bunch. They were always undercover, they kept their own hours and they were constantly exposed to thousands, if not millions, of dollars in illegal transactions. The potential for corruption was overwhelming. They could easily see themselves on a meager cop's salary, even with overtime, against a bunch of low life's engaging in a lavish life style – girl friends, jewelry, family trips, fancy clothes – all thrown in their face on a daily basis. With little or no supervision and a complicit higherup who got a piece of the action, it was very tempting to put some of the drug money in their pockets. The next inevitable step was to have the count of drug packets come up short. The criminals would go to jail anyway. A few short dollars or drug packets wouldn't affect their sentences, and besides, who would believe the drug dealer who tried to rat them out. They were golden, except for one thing: how to sell the drugs. If they sold them back to the dealers, they were in to them forever. They needed an outlet. Avery was ideal. He was small potatoes, he had no backing, no defense. If he was caught by the drug gang dealing for someone else, they would simply eliminate him. The cops would know who did the hit, but they would never want to get too close to the motive. They certainly could never level with the homicide cops doing the investigation. It would be just another internal gang dispute, maybe a hit by another gang. Without the narcotics cops to lay out the background, homicide would never know. And that was the case now. Only I knew the possible motive for the hit. Avery was dealing for the narco cops on the side and he could let homicide know. He could never testify. He had zero credibility now, but he could identify the cops he had been dealing with.   But not now, he was dead. The only evidence they had was a few phone calls to Lt. Keely's daughter, a six year old. I could introduce the few phone calls with some possible drug code messages, but I don't think I could actually prove Avery had the secret connection to the cops. Between the cops themselves, the police union, the City and the D.A. who would be trying the case, they wouldn't need much to belittle my defense. On the other hand, Alison had been caught with what would undoubtedly look like the proceeds from Avery's drug sales, and her prior statements before as to how angry she was on discovering Avery's affair with the Drexel girl while she was supporting him and he was hiding his drug sales from her while he used her money. It was looking like an uphill battle.

The subway came to my stop and I walked over to my office building, still in mid ponder. I did have some friends left – Flacco and the Phantoms.   They had great stuff on the Dogs. Maybe they had some dirt on the narco cops. No harm in asking. Now, how to find Flacco.

As I was going up the elevator, I tried to remember where and when I had seen Flacco. He had always contacted me – at the deli, in my office, but I never knew where he could be found. Then I remembered. The rave.   He had been selling at the rave and wanted to get Avery's spot. With Avery gone, he would try to get that college market. So, get Carmen and go to the rave. See if he was there. Yes, he would help me. If he could get some dirt on the cops investigating him that would be big for him.

As I walked down the hallway to my office, I told Carmen we would be going to look for Flacco. Angelina overheard this. "But, Peter, the rave building was shut down by Licenses and Inspections and padlocked by the Liquor Control Board."

"Oh yes, of course. That would happen."

Carmen said, "Somehow I think Flacco or one of his guys will be hanging around the building looking to pick up drug sales."

"Good thinking. It can't hurt to stroll over there and look for one of the Phantoms."

"Now, Peter, you look too much like a cop. You come with me but sit in the car and stay out of the way."

"I don't know, Carmen. It could be dangerous."

"I'll be just some Penn student looking to score a bag. They won't hurt me. It's bad for business. Then I'll ask to meet Flacco."

"Ok, but I'm bringing a gun."

"Alright, but don't shoot me." So Carmen got into her jeans and a Drexel sweatshirt and sneaks. I got my car out of the garage and dropped Carmen off on Market Street, a few blocks from the rave building. I was sure Carmen could pick out a dealer and then engage him in Spanish. I followed later in the car and parked within eyesight of her.

She walked up Lancaster Avenue a few blocks from the rave. We knew the dealer had to be Hispanic if he worked for the Phantoms.

Soon, she stopped at a car and appeared to be having a brief conversation with the men in an old Camero with a new paint job. Then I heard a knock on my side door window. I jumped out of my skin. It was Flacco.

"Aye Mr. Stern. What are you and your little helper doing here?"

I knew Flacco was no dummy, but I hadn't expected him to keep an eye on the new location.

"So, Flacco, how are you doing?"

"Mas fino. Now what can I do for you?"

"Get in Flacco, let me collect Carmen. I'd like to talk. Is that ok?"

"Sure, Mr. Stern." I started the engine and pulled over to where Carmen had approached the Camero.

"Carmen, come on over and get in." She trotted across the street and got in the back.

There was a rapid exchange of Spanish between Flacco and Carmen. "So, your girlfriend got arrested for offing Andy."

I was about to tell him she was not my girlfriend, but Carmen quickly interrupted. "I told him you were lovers and that you had to protect her. Spanish men get the whole rescue picture."

"Ok, Flacco, you got the picture. So Andy was dealing on the side for these narco cops with their stash of confiscated bags. The Dogs didn't know it."

Another rapid exchange in Spanish. "I explained that Andy was cheating on your girlfriend, and she got caught getting a gym bag out of a health club in the northeast. The homicide cops like her for his murder. We like the narcotic cops for getting rid of someone who might roll over on them. I asked him if he could help."

Flacco turned to look at me. "You know, Mr. Stern, I speak very good English."

"I think Carmen was just showing off. So can you help?"

"We certainly know the narcotics cops in the district are dirty and were connected with the Dogs. They are no friends of ours.

"Ok, so far so good. Now, if you bring them down, you have an open territory until new cops are appointed. And any testimony they might give would be unreliable. Every one of yours that got arrested could walk."

"True, but who can we trust?"

"I've got a guy from Internal Affairs interested. I would trust him with anything. Lt. Mehle."

"Yeah, I heard of him."

"Ok, so what do we do?"

"First, I need to convince Lt. Mehle that the narco cops here are bad."

"No sweat there. We got CD's and other stuff."

"Can you get a box of duplicates like you did before?"

"I gotta talk to the boss, but I'm sure he'll go for it."

"Call me on my cell when you're ready."

"Got it."

"Good." He got out and went over to the Camaro. I drove Carmen back to my garage.

So far so good.

After she had been arrested, Alison was fired from her job so she had plenty of time to see me.

At 9:30 promptly, she came to my office. I could almost hear Angelina snarl as Alison walked past her and into my office. She had had a hair appointment and had nice makeup on. I'm not sure what character she thought she would play for me, but she had on a very short tight skirt and a tight blouse, very business-like. She sat and waited for me to say something.

"So, Alison, you look nice."

"It's Aliyah. So you like the corporate look. I wish I'd known."

"Ok Aliyah. Did you do it?"

"Did I kill Andy? No way. I hate guns."

"But by then you hated Andy."

"True. But I knew if he ever got caught he would be in prison for a long time. So why kill him? Let him find a boy friend in the hoosegow. Besides, when I saw that bimbo he was shtupping after I had been supporting him, I can tell you it was over."

"Ok, the money."

"Well, as you know, I'm no dummy. When I heard how much he had been selling for both the Dogs and the cops, I did the math. I found only $30,000 or so he had stashed in the apartment and knew that wasn't enough. So, I went through all his things. I still didn't find anything. So I went through my things and found a locker key with the logo of the gym in the northeast. It was hidden in back of the frame of a watercolor in the paper backing. So I went out there and sure enough there was a gym bag with lots of dollar bills in it."

"But if you left it there, he might come by and take it one day. He would find the key in the picture frame missing and figure you found it."

"So I filled my own gym bag with as many bills as I could. Mostly 100's and 20's and kept them. I put his gym bag back in the locker and decided to wait until he was arrested or had disappeared for a while. I put his gym bag back in the locker and I put the key back inside the backing of the watercolor."

"So I had a duplicate key made and put the old one back. When Avery took his things and the watercolor with the key, I almost died. If he found anything missing, I figured let him look. Let him come after me. I had the cops on speed dial. And I could let the bag stay in the locker until he was caught. I did take some of the bills, but left most."

"Ok, good so far. But you heard he was dead so you went for the bag."

"Yes. So how did I get caught?"

"The cops found the key inside the picture frame and traced it to you when you claimed it in my office."

"Oops."

"Then, they staked out the gym to see who would claim the bag. They knew you now had access to the key and suspected you of Avery's murder.

"But I didn't do it. Why kill him if he was going to jail?"

"Maybe since he was on the run, he would come back and get the money out of the locker."

"So when you heard he was dead for a while, you decided it was time to take the bag from the locker?"

"That's right. If the cops hadn't recognized me and put two and two together, I would have the bag."

"I see. I see."

"Ok, where were you when he was killed?"

"I don't know when he was shot, but I work from 9 to 5 and I have a half hour subway ride each way. The rest of the time, I am home alone. I might add Peter, I am lonely and single."

"Yes . . . yes. Aliyah, that's out. Ok, so if I know when he was shot, we may have an alibi. That's good. Now, I have to tell the D.A. if I have an alibi defense before trial. It's the law. So I'll get an affidavit typed up and send it to the D.A. Once that is in their hands, they may review the case and drop it. It's all circumstantial now." So I dictated an affidavit for Angelina to type up. She was on it like white on rice and brought our office notary in to witness Alison's signature. She signed both names to the affidavit.

"So that's it, I guess, Peter." She stood up, smoothed her skirt and when Angelina was gone, she gave me a hug as I walked her out the door.

I sent the alibi affidavit to Lou Dawson and requested a meeting. The next day, the dreaded Ms. Liederkranz called me. "Mr. Stern, we've reviewed the affidavit. When can you come to talk?"

I was over in the D.A.'s office that afternoon. I hoped Lou Dawson would be there and mirabile dictu, he was.

"Peter, good to see you."

"Yes, Lou, always good to work with you."

"So the affidavit you sent over covers the probable time of the shooting. Of course, she could have hired someone to do it. Always a possibility, but I've ruled that out." One look at Ms. Liederkranz and I could tell she had not.

"The rest of the case is pretty circumstantial. I am suggesting that, for now, we drop the homicide case. We can always bring it again."

"That's great, Lou."

"If we get some more evidence, we can still arrest her."

"I'm aware of that. What about the gym bag with the money?"

"Well, Peter, it is certainly suspicious. At trial, we prove Witherspoon was a drug dealer, could have had a secret stash, and the key to the locker in the gym came from behind a picture frame in Ms. Rosen's apartment. Just very suspicious.

"All possibly true. I won't get into the defenses yet. But the case sounds weak."

"So we could be open to a plea, if the murder case is dropped."

I thought Ms. Liederkranz would have a cow with all this plea talk, but she kept her peace.

"Ok, Lou. Let's talk when you know more about the murder case."

"Good deal, Peter. I'll let you know."

When Lou Dawson decided to drop the homicide charge until more evidence might come in, the only remaining issue was the gym bag Alison was seen removing from a gym locker. The homicide cases were listed on a separate calendar from the rest. So the preliminary hearing for the gym bag was rescheduled to another date. Now, at a preliminary hearing, it is the prosecutor who must demonstrate to a lower level judge that there is sufficient evidence to move forward with a case to trial. The defense usually only uses these hearings to get as much information about the case as he can. It is his chance to see what the witnesses will say against his clients at the time of trial.

So the hearing was set for a Wednesday. Because it had gotten some media attention, there were a few reporters in the gallery. I, of course, wanted to make the most favorable impression so Alison would get a good review. Of course, I lectured her on the need to be presentable. She listed her wardrobe. She would be a nerd – white blouse, dark blue cardigan sweater, long wool skirt and low pumps. Makeup was an issue. She felt she had to be somewhat attractive, with at least some eye liner and lipstick. I went with that, so she added some reading glasses with wire rims.

I reviewed my notes and jotted some lines of questioning on my legal pad. It was beginning to seem that there might be some holes in the entire case, so I starred and highlighted some of the better issues. Then my heart sank. Judge Theodore was to be the judge for the hearing and Martha Liederkranz the Assistant DA. Judge Theodore was an old political hack who had survived in the political system for decades by doing nothing contrary to his party's interest. In addition to being stupid and lazy, he always followed the DA's lead in cases since that was the easiest and required the least thought. Most judges in Pennsylvania are elected, which means the ward leaders get together and horse trade their choices for judge. Since Theodore was head of some do-nothing agency, the party wished to kick him upstairs to a judgeship. He was an afterthought on a ballot of eleven city judge vacancies. He had now been sitting in total mediocrity for 15 years and he was to be my judge.

The day of the hearing arrived, so Alison and I arrived at 9:00 a.m., but Carmen and Angelina came too. Dr. and Mrs. Rosen sat together with them.

I felt that there were some good issues I could explore so I had researched the law on those issues and had paper clipped pages in the heavy books which reported past opinions to back up my position.

Ms. Liederkranz also came in with a younger assistant D.A. and an entourage of policemen who might be expected to testify. More curious onlookers also filed into the courtroom.

Although the court proceeding was expected to start at 9:30,

Judge Theodore came in at 10:30. The court crier opened court and called Ms. Liederkranz.

"What have you got for us today, Martha?" The judge asked.

"Your Honor, we have a receiving stolen property case and an aiding and abetting drug sales case against Ms. Alison Rosen."

"And you, sir."

"Yes, Your Honor. I am Peter Stern, counsel for Ms. Rosen."

"Very well, proceed Ms. Liederkranz."

The first witness was Detective Sargeant Hembocher. He described how several police officers had staked out the gym in the northeast at a certain locker No. 316. He explained that the key to that locker had been found inside the paper backing of a framed watercolor painting that was inside a van registered to Avery Witherspoon. The police had taken the key to the locker at a gym whose logo appeared on the key. Once inside the locker, they found a gym bag with $301,080 in small bills. The locker key had been issued to Avery Witherspoon, who had recently been found shot in a room at an industrial building at 3908 Lancaster Avenue.

I had been busy taking notes and let the detective ramble on, but enough was enough. I objected. "Your Honor, this is all hearsay and speculation."

"Which part Mr. Stern?"

"The detective observed the stakeout of locker 316, he observed that. Why they did that and the whole warrant business is hearsay and speculative."

"OK, I rule the detective may say what be observed at the stakeout, not why they were there. Proceed detective."

"So we observed Ms. Rosen enter the premises. And she went to the locker and pulled out the gym bag."

"This one?" asked Ms. Liederkranz.

"Yes, the one on property receipt 317266."

"What was in it?"

"Cash, in small bills, neatly wrapped in an amount in excess of $300,000."

"Was a count made on the spot in your presence?"

"Yes. It came to $301,080. We have the exact amount of the property receipt."

"So you arrested Ms. Rosen?"

"Yes, she was arrested."

"Alright, Mr. Stern, your witness."

"Whose gym bag was it, detective?"

"Mr. Witherspoon's."

"How do you know that?"

"The locker was registered to Mr. Witherspoon."

"The only key you had was for locker 316? So that is the only way you knew about the locker, isn't that so?"

"Yes. Later we ran fingerprints. His were on it. Mr. Witherspoon died three days earlier."

"Who else's fingerprints were on the gym bag?"

"Ms. Rosen's."

"Ms. Rosen and Mr. Witherspoon lived together off and on, did they not?"

"Yes."

"So the bag could be Ms. Rosen's as well, couldn't it?"

"I suppose."

"So she may have been retrieving her own bag and her own money."

At this, Ms. Liederkranz jumped up. "Your Honor, we object." Judge Theodore looked puzzled. "So Ms. Liederkranz, how can you tell who this belonged to?"

"May I make an offer of proof." She was offering to explain the whole case to the judge so he could see how it fitted together. I had no objection, since this offer would lay out their whole case for us. The courtroom was abuzz.

"Ok, Your Honor. The The story goes back to when we found Mr. Witherspoon dead of a small caliber gunshot wound. We looked for and found his van. It was loaded with a variety of possessions. Since he was dead, we catalogued the possessions and gave them to Mr. Stern, who represented Mr. Witherspoon, to arrange for them be claimed by his heirs."

"Rather than draw this hearing out, Your Honor, I will stipulate to that as stated. However, for the purpose of this hearing only, we will object to the ownership of one object – a framed watercolor painting."

"Is that acceptable, Martha?"

"Yes, judge. Now, before we turned these items over to Mr. Stern, we of course examined them. Behind the paper backing of the watercolor painting, there was a locker key. We discovered the gym where the locker was located and sealed the key back behind the painting."

"Your Honor, I will also stipulate to that."

"Thank you, Mr. Stern." All this discussion was being

recorded and was now official and part of the court record.

"Proceed"

"We asked Mr. Stern to distribute the items found in Mr. Witherspoon's van to his heirs. Some police went to Mr. Stern's office where he had invited Mr. and Mrs. Witherspoon and Ms. Rosen to claim the items which we had packed in a box. None of the items seemed to have much value, sentimental or monetary, but Ms. Rosen chose the watercolor and the rest Mr. Stern was directed to give to charity."

"So far, I agree as stated. Except I object that the watercolor was Avery Witherspoon's. The police had no power to distribute it."

The judge sat up and Ms. Liederkranz jumped. "How can you say that?"

"Remember, Ms. Rosen is a commercial artist. She went to art school with the woman who painted the watercolor. This woman can so testify and a letter giving the painting at the time to Ms. Rosen is in our possession. It is what is called a provenance and proves Ms. Rosen's ownership. We offer the letter into evidence as Exhibit D-1."

Ms. Liederkranz was quiet for a while. "Alright, the ownership of the painting is irrelevant. It was in Mr. Witherspoon's van."

"True, but if he intentionally or inadvertently took it when he moved out of the apartment he shared with Ms. Rosen, it is still Ms. Rosen's. He knew the locker key was behind the picture frame."

"So what? The key to the locker was sealed in the back."

"Also true, but to breach the back of Ms. Rosen's painting required a search warrant if it was Ms. Rosen's property."

"For several minutes, there was silence. Ms. Liederkranz

asked permission to explain this turn of events to her office and asked for a recess. I was excused by Judge Theodore. I sat back in the courtroom and explained what had happened to Carmen, Angelina and the Rosens. Mrs. Rosen said, "Yes, that watercolor was in our house when Alison lived there. It was a gift from Julia Cooper. Alison had it framed back then."

"Thank you, Mrs. Rosen. If necessary, you could testify to that." It took at least a half hour for Ms. Liederkranz to return.

"Judge, it is clear that Mr. Stern cannot raise search and seizure issues at a preliminary hearing."

This was something the judge did know. At this level, these motions to exclude evidence had to be taken up at a higher level. "I agree, Ms. Liederkranz, the circumstances of the key can come into evidence. So proceed."

"Once the police had the key, they duplicated it, resealed the backing to the painting and turned everything over to Mr. Stern for distribution."

"Did they ever go to the locker and open it?" I asked.

"Yes. Mr. Witherspoon was dead and there was no need for a warrant."

"So you knew the bag was in there and never got a warrant?"

"No, Mr. Witherspoon was dead by then."

Ms. Liederkranz was beginning to get the idea of the search and seizure issue I was raising. I explained to the Rosens, Angelina and Carmen that the police may not enter a person's house, or any closed pieces of property without probable cause. If there is time, the police must obtain a warrant.

"Your Honor, may I have a brief recess so I can get an expert in search and seizure law to hear this matter?"

"No objection, Your Honor."

"Granted. I will get my law clerk as well. Break for lunch. Court resumes at 1:00 p.m.

I wanted to go over my notes so I got a tuna sandwich and a diet Snapple at one of the food trucks and went back to a small conference room off the courtroom. Angelina and Carmen came in quietly later and sat. I ran through the research I had done earlier at 11:55. I got up as Angelina and Carmen looked up at me with inquisitive looks. They knew better than to break my concentration. The Rosens were all sitting in the front row as the court personnel began to filter in. At 1:30, Judge Theodore took the bench. At the District Attorney's table, Ms. Liederkranz and her assistant had been joined by Alistair Sweeney, an Assistant D.A. that handled research and appellate work. We nodded and sat.

"Are we ready counsel?" Judge Theodore glared at us. He was not used to handling difficult matters and looked as if he had a briefing from his law clerk that confused him.

Ms. Liederkranz stood and recalled the homicide detective. He had already been sworn. "So detective, you said you retrieved some items from a van registered to Mr. Witherspoon."

"Yes."

"You examined them, including a watercolor picture where you found a key to a gym locker sealed behind paper backing to the frame."

"Yes."

"I object Your Honor. We asked that you suppress the evidence of the key since he obtained no search warrant to breach the paper behind the frame."

The judge turned to his law clerk and held a conversation in whispers. "For now, I will allow the detective to proceed subject to later adjudication."

"Continuing objection." "Granted."

"The key had a gym logo and a number. So we went to the gym and looked in the locker so numbered."

"Again without a warrant." "Yes, counsel."

"Proceed."

"There was a gym bag in the locker which, by later count, turned out to have over $300,000 in it. We replaced the bag in the locker."   We attempted to put a surveillance camera on the locker but were informed that cameras are not allowed in gym locker rooms. So we resealed the locker key in the picture frame and included it in the items returned to Mr. Stern for distribution at his office.   When Avery Witherspoon's parents and Ms. Rosen came to Mr. Stern's office, we attended. Ms. Rosen was the only one who selected the watercolor."

"We returned to the gym and had the locker staked out. Eventually, Ms. Rosen came to the locker and pulled out the gym bag. She was arrested at that point."

I rose again. "Your Honor, the key is the key. If the police had not found the key behind the paper backing to the picture frame, they would not have known about the gym locker." I could see Alistair Sweeney holding his head in his hands and mumbling something to himself.

"Your Honor, the evidence of the key must be suppressed since the police entered Ms. Rosen's picture frame without a warrant. The key is then traced to the locker, the locker to the gym bag. The gym bag is connected to the stakeout and from there to Ms. Rosen."

Sweeney's mumbling became more audible. I could distinctly hear the words "fruit of the poisonous tree."

"Yes, Your Honor, as the prosecution now realizes, the key connects to Ms. Rosen's arrest. The entire chain of evidence is called the "fruit of the poisonous tree." A constitutional doctrine that says that once a piece of evidence is improperly obtained by a warrantless search, it and any subsequent evidence which is recovered must be suppressed."

Ms. Liederkranz turned on Alistair Sweeney and glared at him. The judge looked imploringly at Ms. Liederkranz. What did all this mean?

Ms. Liederkranz asked the judge for some time to confer with Mr. Sweeney. I had no objection. I and my little entourage walked out to the hallway as Ms. Liederkranz and Mr. Sweeney went into a conference room.

After at least a half hour, the court crier came out to get us. We filtered back into the courtroom and took our places. The judge was already on the bench and Ms. Liederkranz was seated along with Mr. Sweeney."

The judge said, "Mr. Stern, I believe Ms. Liederkranz has a motion to make." "Yes, Your Honor, we withdraw the charges against Ms. Rosen."

My entourage all looked up at me to see what this meant. I knew the withdrawal of charges did not mean the matter was over. They could always bring it back if they ever had more evidence.

"So, Your Honor, you will not rule on suppressing the evidence?" "No, Mr. Stern."

"And the charges may be brought again." "As far as I know, Mr. Stern."

"In that case, I would ask that the notes of testimony and the entire court record be transcribed at my expense." I wanted to be sure that everything would be retained in case they tried to rearrest Alison.

"So ordered." The judge banged the gavel and left. Ms. Liederkranz studiously ignored me as she packed up her papers.

Meanwhile, Alison threw her arms around my neck, tears streaming down her cheeks, "Peter, thank you, thank you, thank you."

While Alison still clung to my neck, I shook Dr. Rosen's hand. Angelina and Carmen were already being interviewed by the press media. Eventually, we could pack up our books and papers in the rolling suitcase.

Freed from the crush of reporters, Angelina and Carmen took the suitcase back. I saw Ms. Liederkranz begin to pack up the gym bag exhibit and the stacks of bills.

"Uh, Martha, I believe that belongs to us." I gestured to the stacks of money "We'll see about that!" She snapped.

Alison turned to me. "You mean that could all be mine."

"I believe so." I knew that the senior Witherspoons could claim it as part of Avery's estate, but the District Attorney could well argue it was the proceeds of drug dealing and, therefore, confiscated. Without that, Alison could simply claim it was in her possession. We'd have to see how that all came out.

That night, at dinner, my wife Lynn asked how did my day go. She sat patiently through a long explanation. My daughter asked if she had to know all this if she was to be a lawyer.